OMEGA

OMEGA

D. Brian Plummer

COCH-Y-BONDDU BOOKS

First published by The Boydell Press 1984
Reprinted by Coch-y-Bonddu Books 2002
© 1984 David Brian Plummer
All rights reserved

ISBN 0 954 2117 1 5

To Ann McDade:

Mistress of tact and diplomacy

Published & distributed by
COCH-Y-BONDDU BOOKS
MACHYNLLETH, POWYS, SY20 8DJ
Tel 01654 702837   Fax 01654 702857

Introduction

How to start this book is the problem, though the ending is all too painfully obvious even as I write. For thirteen years I've hunted David's farm, thirteen of the happiest years of my life, thirteen years marred only by my failure to cope with my job as a teacher. Now in three weeks the farm will be shut down, the buildings sold, the meal sheds emptied and the rats will go. For a while they'll hang around, possibly because there'll be dribbles of meal there for a month or two, but after that—nothing; and my life will take on the same meaningless note it had before I met David. The starting of this book will be difficult, the end all too damnably easy.

I wonder whether ghosts, spirits, auras—call them what you will—linger when people, or even beasts, which have spent a happy time in a certain place, die. Tales are told of boarding houses, dingy, dreary places, homes for the temporary, the outcasts, the misfits, which echo with happy laughter each Christmas, laughter which is a ghostly relic of a time when the house was the home of some happy family of teenagers. When the housing estate has overwhelmed David's plot and the mealshed is a desirable executive four-bedroomed house with all mod cons, will the tenants remark on the ghostly barking that begins at 10.20 and ends just before dawn? Will they be alarmed on the quiet murmuring canine sobs of San, the babblings of a frustrated Climber, the murderous low moans of Jade. I wonder whether Chance's high yikkering bark will sound beneath some living room as prosperous Daddy puts away the Rolls and Mummy greets him with a dry martini.

Enjoy your estate, folks; glory in your £84,000 desirable dwellings suitable for the man who has made it, but remember one thing, a man who didn't make it—a wild-looking chap with hangdog looks, uncombed hair, ill-fitting clothes—had some happy times on this four acres of land that will soon be dotted with box-like houses; and perhaps around midnight some curious and out-of-place quote from Shakespeare will mingle with the ghostly barks and squeals of dogs and rats long dead.

Omega grew into a scrawny sapling.

Early Beginnings

I suppose I've always been keen to have a breed of dog called after me—and the 'Plummer terrier' does sound good, I admit. After all, Wellington had a boot called after him, Davy had a lamp. Admittedly, Thomas Crapper, the inventor of the first self-flushing lavatory didn't come off so well, but then you can't win them all, can you? However, Plummer terrier sounds great, and who knows, when my shabby funeral procession of shabby mourners ambles down to Lichfield, and I am hurriedly shuffled into a shabby grave because my mourners' ferrets are getting restless, perhaps these brown and white bull terrier-headed psychopaths I've set out to breed will be called Plummer terriers. Forty years from now, maybe letters to *The Field* or *Country Life* will discuss what the real Plummer terrier was, and whether Omega's complete collar or Beltane's broken white markings constituted the real pattern for the Plummer terrier. Perhaps some lunatic will claim that the real Plummer terrier had a shilling-sized hole right through the skull, to allow the ever-dripping water that characterises the spots where I usually seem to hunt, to drain through their heads. They are probably right. Another will probably write how I bought my first terrier from an Oxford milkman called Trump—not the dog, the milkman—while I was in between teaching jobs, trading him for two cast-off girlfriends and a greyhound. What the heck, it happened to Jack Russell so why not to me. Then perhaps I can look down from that great rat-infested poultry farm in the sky and mouth, 'Ask Winch, you fools, or seek out Mo, he'll tell you.' Better still I'll write it down and let it be known that this urgent need for immortality, this desperate conceit, rather than my desire to write about Omega, has prompted me to write this book.

Matthew Chapter One starts out with the pedigree of the most famous carpenter's son of all time, starting with Abraham tarrying a bit during the time of bondage (a word which has a somewhat different meaning these days) and finishing up with Joseph. Maybe I'll trace the ancestry of Omega this way, starting at the beginning or dallying awhile at my incarceration in Holmes Rotherham, and finishing up with Vampire, the father of Omega. If you're religiously inclined and find such analogy offensive, then all I can say is 'Tough'—that's the way all pedigrees run, and I'll even be explicit on the dam line which is more than Matthew does. So skipping further impiety, we'll begin with the pedigree because without it no one is going to follow the story which goes back even before my birth. I'll end at Omega as that's the title of the book, but like a ring (with luck) a pedigree too has no end.

```
                    Laddie              The Hackett White
          Vampire <                Tarka <
         /          \ Jennie     /
Omega <                          \ Thistle
         \          Vampire
          Janey  <            Rupert
                  \ Bunty <            Rupert          Scamp
                          \ Janet <          Pig <
                                   \ Jade <     \ Tuffy
                                          \ Spidey
```

    OK. Let's find a starting point. Scamp and Tuffy seem an obvious kick-off so I'll start elsewhere, for no-one can ever call me logical. Since childhood I'd kept a rip-roaring bunch of valley-bred terriers, game as pebbles, ugly, rough coated, prone to mange (and bad mange at that), apt to remain silent underground, particularly if hurt. San was the best of them, the best all-round dog I've ever owned, a dog which ratted with the best of them, bolted fox if he could, slew them if they refused to bolt, stayed well to badger right up until he became doddery, worked otter, dropped to shot, retrieved to hand, and (if I'd decided to teach him) would have performed circus tricks like a poodle. He hated small children as I do, and bred absolutely nothing of any worth when mated to some of the very best bitches in Britain. Ward of Consett would question that, as some of his top strain of red Lakeland owes at least a line to him. Somehow the vital ingredients in the genetic crucible came together with him, but the elements dispersed in his children. I kept several until they were senile and realised that he bred two types of offspring, indifferent and completely useless. Subsequently I looked around for new blood, blood of a tried and tested strain and eventually I settled on a bitch bred by John Cobby's Pickaxe, which brings us to square one of the pedigree, namely a black and white, rough coated long backed bitch called Tuffy. End of San, beginning of the new strain.

I had few regrets about letting the old strain pass into extinction—though it didn't exactly pass into extinction, it merely slumbered awhile, only moved along a different evolutionary line, only to reappear again much later on, but I'm jumping the gun once again. Tuffy was the *beau ideal* of the working terrier, game but sensible, willing to stay to fox or badger practically forever, capable of keeping out of the way when a fox decided to mix it or a badger moved forward at her. She took perhaps only five or six bad bites in her life—as far as I know that is, for a badger eventually proved her undoing. That, however, is really jumping the gun just a bit. Her nose was phenomenal and almost the equal of a hound's. One day she ran a roe, by scent, pulling it down against a thicket, holding its hindlegs without quite knowing why, hanging on like grim death and waiting for me to come up and help, just hoping I'd come and finish off the beast, and when I let the poor wide-eyed prey go, choking Tuffy off while the deer kicked eight bells out of me, Tuffy ran it again for a full five hours, hunting it like a hound, baying and screaming in frustration when it leaped ditches and hedges. She was a lucky purchase, a chance buy, yet she proved the ideal start for my blood line.

Looking back at that damned pedigree, remembering the ghosts of dogs long past, I feel old. It all seems so long ago, yet I still avoid travelling near the canal bank where Tuffy and Stealer, her granddaughter went to ground and never came out of it. Premature burial is a hell of a death, not just for an Edgar Allan Poe, but for a terrier. What happens is, that a terrier goes to ground, finds a cub (or worse still a rabbit) up a small gallery and begins to dig to it. Soon there is earth aplenty thrown behind the terrier and not a great deal of air in front—and the end is obvious. I often wonder whether terriers panic as the air begins to run out, or maybe the murderous enthusiasm which seems to propel a terrier through life, continues until the finish when asphyxiation, or heart failure, brings an end to it all. Every time I read of an unsuccessful Fell and Moorland rescue, I can't help thinking of poor old Tuffy and Stealer suffocating in that badger sett in Wall.

We had bolted fox from that canal bank for two years without a problem, using the one and two-eyed setts as training places for terrier puppies. True, Tuffy had lain up there for three hours one winter morning, entering the earth at nine and being dragged out at noon by a team of so called fellow hunters just before twelve o'clock opening, a time when all fine weather time hunters downed tools and hightailed it to the alehouse, but no-one had ever considered Wall canal earths to be anything more than a temporary sanctuary for foxes. Well, on the day in question, Hemming, and a few other genuine hunters, not the sort to quit when it rained or, 'the wife said I have to be home by four o'clock to look after the kids', took Tuffy, her wild but very glamorous grand-daughter Stealer and three puppies to try for a fox at Wall: a certain 'find' on a crisp January morning. I bemoan certainties today, avoid like a plague a friend who borrows fifty pounds to put on a horse that is a certainty and instantly cry off one-eyed setts known to be safe. The Wall earths were safe, but they did for poor Tuffy and Stealer.

So we jump back awhile to follow the pedigree, actually to the dump where I lived in a two up and two down shack in Rotherham, and a bit further back besides to the time when I was waiting for my house to become vacant and shared a shed next to Holmes graveyard with my dogs. Talk about *I Walked by Night*—the Rider Haggard hero wouldn't have a look in, eccentricity wise. Rabbits abounded, living mostly under old gravestones, and in a good year I ferreted more rabbits from under 'He Sleeps with the Angels' and 'More Blissful is death than life', than I took off the whole of the Barrows shoot when I poached it for spite twelve years ago, and while I broke my leg falling into a newly-dug grave while chasing rabbits by moonlight with a pack of ghostly terriers and a whippet, all in all I enjoyed Rotherham.

At that time some of the best terriers in Britain—and I mean best from the point of view of work, as I dislike show-bred terriers and the rather nasty bad feeling which pervades most shows—were bred by Eric Taylor who lived (and still does; I saw him six weeks ago) in a tiny village near Derby—a spit from where Mo lives, now that he is between jobs. Taylor had two terriers at the time, a small, short-legged bitch called Jill with the nose of a hound and a leggy prick-eared dog called Mick who expressed his pleasure at first seeing me by sinking his teeth through the calf of my leg and trying to shake off a sizeable piece of meat. Eric watched without emotion and simply said, 'You know he's never done that before—I suppose he can spot a bad'un on sight,' and then made me tea while I mopped up my bleeding and aching leg.

Two pups came out of the union of mating the Taylor-bred Scamp (a Mick and Jill union offspring), an ugly prick-eared heller of a dog, bad with children and adults alike, but a dog whose courage knew no bottom and could hunt like a hound to Tuffy. The first was a white dog I called Pig (he snorted and snuffled every time he was pleased to

A terrier show.

see me), a white-bodied dog which resembled one of those old English white terriers used in catch weight rat contests. Pig killed rats gleefully and gobbled them up equally gleefully—a quality all the pack seemed to have inherited. His sister Clown was prick-eared, and had a white clown's patch over one eye. Both however had the same peculiarity— a curious flaw in their makeup which may have been a fault in their training as much as a genetic abnormality. Both would stay forever to badger, fencing just out of range, baying like thunder and never chancing a grappling match. They'd remain like this until the digger crowned through to them, and were totally steady and sane when I bagged the badger. After that, things went a bit out of kilter I suppose, for once a single badger had been removed from the sette, neither Pig or Clown would go back for another, and when encouraged to go back into the sett, would simply go back to the bagged badger and bay at the sack. Pig died of old age; Clown suffered a less pleasant fate, I suspect.

    I was on my uppers at the time and that's putting it mildly, and getting to accept the stark penury of my life as normal. Clown had whelped a litter of puppies to San on my kitchen floor, and I was beginning to tolerate the awful acrid smell of birth and puppy rearing, though I've never kept dogs in the house since. Well, the pups grew to five weeks old and looked first rate when tragedy struck in the form of three Welsh idiots sent me by Bill Brockley. At that time Bill sent any fools, time wasters and pompous lunatics straight down to my place, where they spent a fairly happy time wasting a day or maybe even two or three, leaving without buying a puppy, using my studs without even saying thank you. That's life, I guess, and later I sent a similar crowd of time-wasters to Bill, so I've always regarded it as even and have a soft spot for Bill. This particular day's time-wasters were from near my own home and had all the marks of thief written on them. By this time I had hopped back into teaching once more and although I earned only £60 a month—it cost me £4 a week to bus it to work—school dinners and constant free samples of benzyl benzoate had caused my physical condition to improve out of recognition. Mo talks about the awful starkness of my life when he met me first, but by the time I had teamed up with Mo things were a lot better, believe me, and I didn't consider post-Mo days as being particularly hard. I never needed much, and now as I write this, the eve of my forty-fifth birthday, for the first time in my life I can say I own two pairs of shoes. Meanwhile back to the plot.

The Welsh lads turned up at my shack at 9 a.m. on Sunday—tattoos, untaxed van, slightly macho and with all the signs of first-class time-wasters embroidered on them. Ostensibly they had come to buy a puppy and I admit I did really need the £6 which reasonably good Russell puppies fetched at that time. Anyway they had the marks of time-wasters, and were obviously up from Wales to spend an odd hour or so before the pubs opened. The lead lunatic wanted a puppy or better still—and this is my pet hate—'a dog doing a bit'—a term which sets my teeth on edge as it labels the user as a dolt who is adept at wrecking good terriers and returning them to the seller as useless, broken-spirited and often emaciated beasts. He asked for a trial—which is a bit of a tall order for a puppy of five weeks old—(this confirmed my diagnosis that the chap was a clown) but settled for a chance to watch the parents work. Clown still had milk, so reluctantly I took the fools to a nearby earth, a shallow, easily dug earth which invariably housed a fox, and put Clown to ground. She found instantly and began to bury steadily and sensibly. The time passed and as the hands of the clock limped their way to opening time, the leader of the group began fidgeting and kicking his heels as I waited for Clown to come out. 'We'll see you after 3 p.m.—come back for you,' he shouted as they raced off towards Lichfield. I waited another hour and decided to walk home and get a spade. When I arrived home I realised my would-be clients would not be coming back. They'd gone back to my house, stolen my alarm clock and taken all of Clown's litter apart from Wanton, a small undersized bitch, who became the great-grandmother of Vampire. Later that month they pulled the same stunt on Moss Stevens fifteen miles away. It takes all sorts I suppose, and sadly I trundled back, spade in hand, to dig out Clown. She wasn't in the earth and though I dug until school next morning, and Billy, my constant kennel help, a school governor's son, played truant next day to look for her, Clown had vanished. Had she been picked up by one of the travellers who flock to the district each autumn? Had my fellow countrymen decided to take the dam as well as the puppies? I suppose I'll never know the answer to that one. The story is a bit off-country, I suppose, but it does explain two points: firstly, why I hate the tattoos and earrings brigade, and secondly what a gullible fool I was at that time. Today I lock up my shuttered windows, switch on my alarm system and my house resembles Fort Knox before opening time. In those days I didn't even lock my door before going to school. I've learned the hard way, I suppose. Mo describes my wanderings at that time as 'Gullible's travels' and certainly the number of fiends who fleeced me repeatedly would stretch from Land's End to Spitzbergen, let alone John o' Groat's.

OK so we're back to tracing the pedigree again—and once again feeling extremely old and battered. At that time I made an odd bob or two, and boy do I mean odd, translating old Hebrew documents into English. Now for all those who don't read Hebrew and that must go for the majority of terrier book readers, I suppose, Hebrew is read from right to left not left to right as is English and the reading of Hebrew requires a different approach. Most of the stuff I translated was for historians, though my clients had a liberal sprinkling of madmen among them. One of these madmen lived on the south coast of England and specialised in curious books of spells, the chanting of which enabled a man to turn into a werewolf. It didn't work. I tried it after promising Mo that if it succeeded I'd mate his greyhound bitch to breed a litter of rather unusual lurchers. But as I've said it didn't work.

While down on the south coast I came upon a gamekeeper working a small, rough, tan and white Russell to badger—a single bitch who without quitting, without the dogs to go in at half time, stayed for six hours baying, teasing, holding and emerging without a scratch. To cut a long story short, he'd had the bitch from a woman called Joan Begbie who bred a neat little strain of JRTs descended from Cobby's Pickaxe on one side and Nimrod Capel's Bluecap (1905) on the other. Subsequently I bought a granddaughter of her Seale Cottage Welcome, a fiercely possessive bitch, wicked with cats and so hard she would bite a hedgehog in two at a snap, paying for the puppy with the money from my would-be magician client. Today it is common practice to knock any elderly lady who breeds hunting dogs, as it must seem a little incongruous (that is to say the least) to imagine some of these public and finishing school ladies wielding a spade to get a badger out, or worse still fishing around in a sewer culvert to poke out a rat, but many great hunting dogs have been bred by such ladies. At that time Breach Kennels, owned by a Miss Sixton (I met her once), turned off a whole crop of utterly fearless, self-entering Jack Russells, one of which became an ancestor of Graham Ward's strain of famous working Lakeland terriers. On the subject of working Lakelands, some of the toughest terriers I've ever seen were registered Lakeland terriers bred by Miss Morris of Kelda Kennels in Stroud. Books should never be judged by their covers and many of these ladies were keen, practical geneticists eager to keep the working qualities of their wards. Winch once bought a cracking little Jack Russell from Mrs Nicholson of Taunton, a terrier in no way inferior for the fact that a woman had bred it.

Likewise the Seale Cottage strain of Jack Russell terrier; Joan Begbie had a line supposedly bred down from the dogs of Nicholas Snow infused with some of the best blood in the West country. She kept pedigrees—I still have mine—and used only good quality small males from strains which were worked regularly by 'hunts' and laymen alike. She inbred rather too severely to Welcome, her best bitch, the photograph of which is in the book *Hunting Parson* by Eleanor Kerr; and I owe many of the defects in my own strain when I continued to inbreed, none to wisely I must add, to this self-same bitch. Most were rough-coated, some none too good on the legs I admit, but I think the failure rate of her stock was remarkably small. The bitch I purchased from Miss Begbie was registered in her private stud book Seale Cottage as Saucy. I called her Spidey.

I worked Spidey to just about every British quarry from rabbit to wildcat and had no complaints. She was, I admit, spiteful, a voracious rat eater, prone to cause trouble in the run, but other than that she was the epitome of a good working bitch, eager to please, steady with stock, game as they come, but as sensible an animal as I could want. In her third season she was put to Pig, the Tuffy/Scamp son, and bred four puppies, a rough male, a tiny, almost minute rough coated female called Smally on account of her size, a half-faced bitch of superb type and a long-backed bitch called Jade who became one of the most important brood bitches in the Midlands—no, dammit, in England. I gave Smally to Billy to sell, as the poor lad had not been paid since he came to work with me and had suffered in silence without a single complaint, but he literally blew the sale. A rather fragile, pretty woman recently estranged from her prosperous husband came to the house one day to buy a puppy for her nervous, rather withdrawn girl aged maybe six or seven, and who still had the punch marks of the husband/wife conflict that had preceded the separation. The child hid behind Mummy as Billy tried a sales spiel trying to sell Smally, and persuade Mummy that this diminutive puppy would be a better bet than a Shetland sheepdog. Billy however is no salesman. 'Just look at it,' offered Billy, handing the child the puppy. 'Just handle it.' The child withdrew further into a cocoon of insecurity. 'Mind you,' Billy continued, 'it's a bit small for badger.' The woman's face creased in bewilderment, 'But both sire and dam', Billy went on, 'will have the throat out of a fox in no time flat.' 'I fink it's a Shetland sheepdog for the kid,' sniffed Mo, and the lady left, saying she'd think it over. Obviously she did, for we never saw her again. As it turned out it was a fortunate loss of sale, and I gave Billy my broken motor scooter as payment. A week later some thieves hit my kennels, taking with them Clown (who was quite a young bitch at the time), Smally, Halfface and Ping. They were stopped at the lights by the police. Ping leaped out and was killed by a passing car and the rest went on to be kennelled in a thieves' coal-house for the night. They were recovered next day but even a day is a bit long if the coal-house has held a litter of puppies which had died of distemper. I lost four dogs through the outbreak which was passed on to me with magnificent generosity, four dogs too young to be inoculated. The rough-coated male died in a thrashing fit. Halfface lost the use of her hind quarters and began to drag herself about the place. For a while I thought she might get over it, but after a month the condition worsened and it became all too obvious what had to be done.

On a more cheerful note, Jade didn't even look ill and the diminutive Smally had one slight fit and recovered. She died, aged nineteen, six weeks ago, a crotchety old dame, bad with postmen, evil with children and domineering as only an ancient matron can be. Courage-wise, nose-wise, instinct-wise, she wanted for nothing, and in spite of her frail shape during her fifth season, I decided to breed from her.

Choosing a mate for such a bitch is often a bit o'a problem. True, there are a thousand males being taken around the shows each summer, some worked, some merely pets, and one would do well to ignore some of the outlandish claims made by their owners. 'See this dog'—a battered one-eared veteran without teeth—'took a thousand badgers, yes a thousand.' Chances are that he obtained those hideous scars while trying to avoid a confrontation with a badger, while another dog working behind him pushed the poor devil into Brock, who with some aplomb divested the wretched dog of bottom lips and most of the lower jaw. A good-looking dog, just what I wanted, parades around the show for the judge to examine. 'Don't touch his mouth,' squeals the owner to the judge. Chances are the dog is undershot, a defect which he will pass on to his family in due course as soon as one tends to inbreed that line. Ask a proud owner the ancestry of his very likely looking dog. 'Out of a very good dog, mate,' will be the reply. Pursue the question a little further—'Which dog?' Dollars to doughnuts, the owner will bluster, a little go off the subject, and finally maybe even admit he hasn't a clue which dog. A KC registered breed such as a border or a cairn, and then you've a good idea of the ancestry of the specimen in question—the pedigrees are not infallible, believe me, but with a Jack Russell terrier, choosing a suitable male for stud is often a heck of a problem.

Finally I settled on Micky, a male owned by Charlie Lewis, a good stud, a superb looker, a fine worker and a dog whose ancestry Charlie could trace back maybe forty years. Charlie had been in hunt service for years and had broken his back during a hunting fall, and knew terriers as well as any man alive. I've often wondered what would have happened if I'd mated Smally to another dog, for as luck would have it her first union to Micky resulted in a Caesarian operation, which produced three puppies, two bitches and a small immaculately neat miniature terrier called Rupert—a heavily marked copper, red and white little dog—the first of the heavily marked dogs that were to become my trademark. Rupert was, in fact, the forerunner of the type of dog I one day hope will be called the Plummer terrier.

Rupert was not quite ten inches tall and could be spanned by a small lady's hands. His courage was bottomless, and though his commonsense was questionable, for at six months he took on the ageing San, menacing and putting in snaps and bites until the ugly old devil retaliated as only he knew how, locking in jaw to jaw, holding and shaking the puppy until Rupert's bones rattled. I shouted San off—the only terrier I've ever been able to curb like this, and Rupert, screaming with rage, followed up his attack, only to be trounced again and again. Even at six months old Rupert had a crazy pluck, a sort of suicidal courage he passed on to some of his offspring. In spite of his short temper, his touchy ways and the almost paranoid hatred of anyone in a uniform (he once worked over an A.A. man who was trying to get in some girlfriend's car), he had all the qualities I wanted in a terrier. His incredible nose he passed on to each and every one of his many children. He never bred a quitter in all the time he stood at stud, and finally he was responsible for the breeding of 42 working-certificated offspring. Climber, Coin, Penny, Julie and a host of other bitches at hunt service fourteen years ago were all of his getting, but sadly through Rupert, I met some of the most disreputable characters I have ever met.

To the best of my knowledge I have never been called mean; dirty, lascivious, lazy, incompetent, yes, but never 'mean'. I am however a sucker for a hard luck story and the sight of a child with a dog on leash in a show usually ruins my 'eye' for a working terrier, and you can guess who gets the prize. Sometimes however, one can be too much of a sucker and I sometimes get my fingers quite badly burned for my impromptu generosity. Well, during Rupert's second year at stud when he was known to be breeding pretty fair stuff, to say the least, a team of weirdos arrived from Walsall, a district where I teach at the time of writing and a town which boasts one district which can well be described as a ghetto. My visitors (and boy, I rue the day they came), slurped out of the van like an unpleasant mess of syrup. All were tattooed, some with little stars on their ears, others with earrings (and folks, if you've ever wondered why I just won't have people like this over my doorstep of the cottage, just read on).

There is a superstition about evil never coming over the doorstep uninvited. I'll explain: should Count Dracula, Sawny Bean, Francis Gutteridge or Sweeny Todd ever appear outside your house, you are quite safe unless you invite them in (just in case you know of three of the above and have missed out on Francis Gutteridge, I think it fair to explain, Francis was an army associate of mine who went to zoos to torment the chimpanzees. When they squeezed out something unspeakable to throw at him, Francis would leap behind an old woman who then received the full wrath (and a bit more besides) of the chimps. Indeed, Francis was truly evil. Now this is nothing whatsoever to do with the story, but I knew Gutteridge far better than I knew Dracula, Todd or Bean—now read on).

However, once you made these unspeakables welcome, you were just begging for trouble. I really should have paid more attention to Coleridge's 'Christabel' at school and told these vermin from Walsall to hop it, but I was younger then, more gullible and friendly with people. Boy, oh boy, have I learned my lesson! Hence I invited them in and gave heed to their hard luck stories, giving them two puppies for their sick children or crippled mothers—I forget which. To cut a long story short, I would have done better to encourage Gutteridge to my house, for since that day I have written off a dozen or so puppies a year to these villains, puppies which usually finish up on tinkers' sites rather than at the bedsides of crippled old ladies and sick children. I've secured one or two convictions against these villains and they've been given tiny fines for their activities, but year in, year out, my premises are raided with the same old *modus operandi*, varied only by the occasional onslaught on the house for cameras and jackets (God knows, they must be desperate to steal my clothes).

Second unpleasant oddity about to appear—and a rather nasty one at that. I've never put my dogs at public stud, possibly because I'm not particularly mercenary, but mostly because putting such a dog at stud literally invites weirdos and lunatics to one's house, much as flies are attracted by the proximity of something nasty. Know-it-alls (and the terrier world abounds in instant experts who are buying their first terrier one week and judging the next) will ask for their bitch to be mated 'naturally'—a little game consisting of bitch running loose, screaming and towing the dog around by his genitals—which I must admit wouldn't appeal to me very much. Quaint old ladies who with a total disregard for a breeder's advice insist on mating their bitches to absolutely unsuitable stud dogs are legion, and rogues, quite often army officer and ladies' finishing school types who promise to pay once the bitch has conceived seem to turn up twice daily. Once while mating Twirl, Rupert's son, to a white bitch belonging to a doctor, I had my face savaged by the reluctant matron, and the number of times my hands, feet and legs are savaged seem to be without number.

Training a team to rag.

Worse still, if I offer a dog at stud, or I sell puppies for that matter, I make friends, and as most of the dog breeding world are in a state of matrimonial flux, perched between a marriage and a divorce, I find for some curious reason that I am treated as a sort of father confessor by both husband and wife, told the most outrageous tales of their marital relationships, tales best kept to the bedroom, I must add. Then, when these unhappy people finally kiss and make up, they are horrified to realise that they have blurted out their sexual secrets to a near-total stranger and I never see either partner again. Truly, in the words of the immortal Moses Bernstein, a purveyor of sole, whiting and kosher foods, 'A friend in need is a pain in the arse', but yet once more I am off course again, heading for precisely nowhere.

As I was saying, I never offer my dogs at public stud, but one day a rather down-at-heel, untidy chap plus wife, plus four rather down-at-heel untidy kids, arrived in a Morris Minor van with a rather untidy down-at-heel bitch terrier, 'nearly in season', to use my visitor's words. He explained that he had just paid four pounds for the bitch from some chap or other and he wished to put her in whelp to sell the puppies. He then added that by trade he was a general dealer and needed the money. I sensed he was as hard up as I was and agreed to let Rupert mate the bitch free of charge and I also agreed to keep his bitch in my rather tumbledown kennels for a week or so until she was mated (also free of charge). Bitch to kennels, team out ratting, and returning home I found that the bitch had set to with a vengeance in the kennels, tearing the kennel apart and vanishing into the night.

I was in a hell of a predicament, and I could not see a way out. It was raining, tipping it down so to speak, but I walked the fields in the rain for ten hours, shouting out Tina, Spot, Patch or any of the other names unimaginative people usually call a terrier. I even chanced on a Tiger or so but to no avail—the damned bitch had disappeared into thin air. Next morning I phoned the general dealer, apologetically offering to replace the bitch with a first class puppy, and return him the four pounds he'd paid for her. I was alarmed to find a note of glee in his voice—a sort of 'I've got you now' tone, and he began talking about compensation for the bitch—compensation in the terms of £400–£500, an enormous sum of money ten years ago, and a fairly large sum for me even today. 'You only paid four pounds for her,' I spluttered. 'Yes,' (a note of triumph now), 'but what about the kids who are grieving and the £200 would have made other puppies,' he replied almost jubilantly. I dried my hair, poured the water out of my wellies and sallied forth again out into the rain, but as night fell the bitch was nowhere to be found.

I phoned him again, aware of his glee as he heard my 10ps dropping into the slot. 'Look,' I said weakly, 'I'll give you my best Rupert puppy *and* a young bitch *and* repay you your four pounds'; but he wasn't having any. By now his wife had gone into a state of shock and the kids were pining away until the oldest girl looked like Camille getting ready to snuff it. Furthermore, in the meantime my general dealer had gone round to a solicitor and had been told to ask for at least £800, for loss of dog, grief and loss of income from the puppies. I knew he was lying, but what the heck could I do. I searched for four days, reporting each day and heard the price soar to £1,300 or I'll tell the police. What to do was a problem, and I was preparing to get the hell out of the district when I saw a 'found' ad in our local post office. His bitch had been found by a passer-by and taken to Matlock some thirty-five miles away, by a corgi breeder. Sunday morning I boarded a variety of buses and walked two miles and fetched back the bitch, carrying her back to my cottage through another torrential thunderstorm. I phoned my dealer happily, almost shouting my joy down the phone. He seemed oddly unenthusiastic and dropped his demand to a two hundred quid 'grief money' request.

He fetched the bitch the next day and I threw in a puppy for good measure hoping he'd forget the unpleasantness, and after paying him two pounds for his petrol money (which wasn't in our original agreement if I remember correctly) he left, talking about grief and solicitors, loss of income and solicitors, and just solicitors. I checked my money tin which acted in lieu of a bank account. I had twelve pounds six pence to last a month, and breathing a sigh of relief I went to bed, absolutely exhausted by the havoc this mercenary swine had caused; but there was worse to follow, for once this chap had a hold he latched on like a bulldog.

I had almost forgotten about my extortionist, when six weeks to the day after his bitch had bitten through the shed and escaped, the general dealer turned up at the house to inform me his bitch had produced six black puppies, pedigree unknown, and certainly not sired by Rupert. My money-grabbing lout, who had no idea of genetics and certainly no notion of the gestation period of a dog, then went berserk when I informed him his bitch had been three weeks in whelp when he had bought her; true to form, he rambled into a spiel about damages, loss of income and all the 'usuals' I had come to expect from him. Furthermore, he then consulted a solicitor (who also had no idea of the gestation period for a dog) who turned off a letter asking for a sum of money which rivalled the National Debt. It was like some hideous nightmare with scenario by kind permission of *The Financial Times*.

At that time I worked in a rather prim and proper sec. mod. attempting to masquerade as a comprehensive, and my persecutor knew all about the pretensions of our very respectable headmaster. Thus each and every day the extortionist phoned the head and told him that if I didn't cough up the 600-odd pounds I owed him, he'd go to the police and reveal some hidden secret of mine—he didn't mention which particular secret. My head, like all good, reliable God-fearing headmasters, promptly panicked, and while he didn't exactly ask me to resign, he made it fairly clear that he'd like it if I pushed off to pastures which, while they might not be greener, would be some considerable distance from his school. I spoke to Mo about the whole messy business, which to tell the truth was beginning to break me up a 'mite'. 'Go to Old Bill,' (all policemen are Old Bill to Mo) ' 'and yourself in, and ask to be investigated' was Mo's advice, which seemed incredible at the time, but I did as he asked and the harrassment promptly stopped; but boy oh boy, I never again took bitches in to board while they were waiting to be served—I'm slow to learn but once I have, it sticks.

Rupe caused me no problems. He was a good hunter, a neat keen stud of good type, a bit small for some I admit, as his puppies rarely topped ten inches. I showed three of his puppies at my one and only show, only to be told by the judge, a thickset man from the North, that he considered them too small to be any good for fox. He then went through an elaborate description of what should constitute a suitable terrier for working fox, while I stood by patiently listening to the most utter rubbish imaginable. I just wasn't even considered in the smooth bitch class, and left the ring with my three Rupert bred bitches. Next class was the Working Certificate class—a small class indeed, for it had only three entries—mine! I won first, second and third of course, and since then I have never shown a dog. I gave my three cards to a little girl with buck teeth, glasses and pigtails whose terrier had also been thrown out of the smooth bitch class. A week ago she came to see me. She's a radiantly beautiful woman now and I felt very old remembering Rupert and his progeny.

Rupert, for all his good qualities, might damn nigh bring about the extinction of the strain however. Now when one has a stud one believes to be the bee's knees, it is a hell of a temptation not to inbreed to him. Motcliffe said, I think, that the difference between inbreeding and line breeding is that if one is successful in producing good stock, the genetic programme is called line breeding. If one makes a hash of the whole business and produces weird monstrosities which resemble beasts from an Hieronymus Bosch painting then I'm afraid the genetic programme is called inbreeding. So it can be fairly safely said I inbred to Rupert—and this was a hell of a mistake.

His progeny mated to the San/Clown Pig/Spidey bloodline was incredible. All were nearly identical, all were outstanding workers and every one was nearly a duplicate of the sire. Hence I became tempted and rather unwisely used him a bit more than a corner stone for the strain. I mated him to his daughters, mated his son Twirl to his own half sisters and mated Rupert's grandson, a curious little dog called Thing, to his great grandmother. The result of this genetic mix can best be described as disastrous. I only became aware of the problems when quite a few of the puppies died within five days of their birth, whimpering and bleating their way into emaciated, dehydrated skeletons. I put the loss of the first two litters down to the fact that Jade had twelve puppies in her litter and the devil took the hindmost, but when Worry and Witch, Rupert's two daughters whelped five puppies and two displayed the same symptoms of those in Jade's litter, I decided to look into things. I autopsied the abdomens of the puppies but apart from the fact that the tiny stomachs contained no curdled bitches' milk I found nothing. The heads revealed the answer however for the puppy had no roof to its mouth. This cleft palate gene was now firmly established in the strain, and very few of Rupert's bitches didn't carry this terrible cleft palate problem. One of the only bitches Rupert bred which did not throw cleft palate puppies was Janet, a pale tan and white bitch I gave to an ex-girl friend of mine to fulfil a promise to her infant daughter. Janet was mated to Rupert to prove that she didn't carry the cleft palate gene and bred Bunty, which brings us one step further to the Omega line.

The line was now saturated with Rupert's blood—so much so in fact that I desperately needed an outcross of a similar type, but a million miles away genetically, so once more I began to frequent the shows, listening to the same ghastly lies I heard when searching for a stud to breed Rupert. I went to a dozen shows ranging from gymkhanas in the Midlands which boasted some of the ugliest, fattest terriers imaginable to a Fell and Moorland Show near Scotland, the terriers of which were tall enough and leggy enough to outrun deer let alone work badger. I was beginning to accept the genetic abnormalities of my own strain, when one day luck smiled on me—not a frequent happening these last few years, believe me.

I'd known Jim French for maybe seven or so years since the time when he was terrier man for the Meynell Fox Hounds. In fact I'd given him Coin—a daughter of Jade and Rupert. Jim had an excellent reputation as a terrier man—a good digger and a man who didn't start a terrier too soon or overmatch it too young. Few dogs failed with Jim, but he had itchy feet and rarely stayed long at any hunt. He left the Meynell for the Hampshire Fox Hounds, a spot nearer his place of birth, but somehow the Hampshire didn't suit him and he returned to the Atherstone, only to leave and take up employment with the Cotswold. During his stay at the Meynell, Jim set great store by the dogs of Derek Goddard of the Chiddingfold and Leconfield Fox Hounds and obtained a bitch called Jill from Goddard, a straight-legged, prick-eared bitch sired by Goddard's dog Scrap, a slightly undersized male which did quite a lot of winning at the shows against the then fashionable 14- and 15-inch terriers which won regularly on the show circuit for maybe five years or more. Scrap was a good typey male with a wonderful front, good mouth and a perfect back. On the debit side, he tended to throw a prick ear or so, and a rather curious loose coat, but his stock was peerless in the working field and had a reputation for having an unerring nose, capable of finding a fox in the deepest badger earths in Hampshire.

Jim had lost Jill, his tricolour Scrap-bred bitch, with nephritis, a kidney complaint which often rendered her *hors de combat* after a hard day's work, yet though the flesh was sometimes weak, the spirit was truly great for she would stagger to her feet in an effort to follow Jim when he bundled the terriers into his van. Jim had owned a sister of this bitch and she had had a short but incredibly useful life with the Meynell before her death in a kennel fight (or was it a motor accident? I forget which). Thus it was not surprising that Jim went to Goddard for a replacement—a male called Laddie, a rather washy coloured tan and white, poor coated dog of excellent type and with a marvellous head. What was surprising was the fact that Jim eventually sold the dog to me. On the dam side the dog was impeccably bred, dating from some of Goddard's father's dogs, all of which had seen hunt service and all of which were show stoppers. All in all Laddie took some beating as a potential stud dog. Maybe Jim was between jobs and didn't need a terrier or perhaps he didn't really take a fancy to Laddie. Whatever it was, Laddie changed hands at the age of six months for £15, a considerable sum in those days, but a trifle when one considers that Jim had raised him for six months, inoculated him and started him to fox even at that age. Laddie sired over a hundred puppies all of which would work well and hunted like hounds. Furthermore, in spite of the fact he was a replica of the type I was breeding, with a blanket marked back and tan head, he was not related to Rupert in any way. Thus he didn't carry any of the defects my line carried. On the debit side I always felt his kidneys were a bit suspect—maybe the tendency to develop nephritis is inherited I don't know, and neither does my vet for that matter. He bred poor coats and washy colour with some bitches and I lost the vivid red colour of my strain for a generation or so. What was worse, was that mated to certain related bitches he bred (I'd started to inbreed once again) a curious defect I'd never encountered before, nor have I seen since. Some puppies were born with normal mouths and developed normal deciduous teeth with a level and even scissor bite. The second teeth were a very different matter for only the carnasial teeth came through the gums (and those sometimes irregularly) and the rest of the mouth was a gummy mess with permanent teeth noticeable only by their absence. Believe me, inbreeding is thwart with problems. I stamped out this line, I'm glad to say, though one line to Laddie, which I don't own, still carries this hideous gene.

Meanwhile back at the ranch the San-Clown line liberally sprinkled with Rupert and a dash of Cyril Breay's 'Patterdales' (I hate that name) had bred a neat bitch called Thistle which I mated to a fighting bull terrier called The Hackett White. Thistle was a damned good terrier, honest and eager to work, a bit fiery perhaps and another rat gobbler, but a good worker nevertheless. Thistle lived to a ripe old age and was damned nigh senile before I mated her to the Hackett White and bred a putty-nosed bitch of exceptional type and character which I gave to Audrey, a close friend of a girl friend I had at one time who was so important in my life that I have forgotten her name. Audrey had Jennie as a pet but decided to breed from her. Her first litter to Laddie consisted of two dogs and a bitch. I bought back the bitch, a tan and white puppy which wrinkled its mouth as if to smile if I spoke

Cyril Breay shortly before his death.

Vampire at his murderous best.

to it in a cajoling manner. I have no regrets about buying this puppy for she became Beltane, one of the best bitches I've ever owned.

Her second litter was slightly larger and consisted of two bitches and two dogs. I bought the lot, calling them Vampire, Verdelak (a Russian vampire), Witch and Warlock. They were a fiery bunch out of which only one managed to survive, for Vampire killed Verdelak, Witch and Warlock in kennel fights, grim, silent and very bloody fights with no quarter asked and certainly none given. Warlock was beautiful and at the time of writing I have a puppy which is a duplicate of Warlock, a fine red and tan, blanket marked puppy with heavy dropped ears and a magnificent front. I call him Fat Boy though he is registered as Warlock II.

Vampire continued his line by mating Bunty and producing a bitch I called Samaine after the ancient Celtic winter solstice festival (Beltane = summer, Samaine = winter). Funnily enough, although the bitch was of good type and had pluck and instinct to spare, I just couldn't stand her. She irritated me from the time she left the nest. Maybe as one gets older, small things tend to irritate. I won't have anyone who smokes over the door, and my contact with the Walsall bunch has made me a bit more than apathetic to tattoos and earrings brigade. Likewise certain mannerisms in dogs upset me and upset me so much that it is wise to give a dog displaying such mannerisms to a friend. Dogs which are forever jumping up are favourite hates, as are shy fighters, dogs which run into a corner and snap at the rest of the pack, setting off a hell of a battle; but my extra special, super-duper hate is the foot shuffler, and I'd better explain what that is. I insist on absolute obedience in my terriers during a hunt, and if I tell a terrier to stay by my foot I expect it to comply with my demands to the letter. Samaine did, but she would insist on shuffling her feet as she stood by a rat hole, an irritating habit which began to drive me damn nigh insane as the bitch grew older. True, she was a superb hunter and a wonderful rat killer, but I just couldn't break her of the habit. Each hunt would find her fixed at my feet, shuffling away in anticipation of the rat moving within biting range. Thus, after one particularly annoying hunt, a hunt in which Samaine killed maybe two dozen rats, I gave Samaine away to a nearby dog breeder who promised her a good home. He immediately renamed her Janey for some reason or another, for most Russell breeders are a particularly unimaginative

A catch in the meal shed; Fat Boy third from left.

band as the host of Spots, Queenies, Pips and Floss's at shows attests. A pity that. I think Samaine was a great name, much better than Janey, in fact come to think of it I'd be hard pressed to find a worse name than Janey.

So my breeder brought Janey back for mating as he'd promised, and though he'd set his heart on Warlock siring the litter, Warlock had gone to ground in Broughs Earths and taken a pounding that day and was in little mood for siring a litter, or standing upright for that matter. So Vampire was mated to his own daughter and bred a fairly ghastly crop of puppies only one of which, a tall spidery bitch with huge all-seeing eyes seemed worth keeping. She stepped out of the box and I spotted her instantly taking her in lieu of a stud fee. She was bright, wildly keen, eager to train and frantic to please. Sadly, she was a maddening foot shuffler so at the age of four months old she was given away to a schoolboy as a pet. The schoolboy was Colin Latham. The bitch puppy was called Omega.

Omega

I'd have been £5,200 down in betting money if Omega hadn't been hyperactive, and difficult to kennel, for curiously the same hyperactivity which manifested itself in foot shuffling and caused me to part with Omega, caused the young Latham to return her the next day. Omega had been a devil to kennel as a puppy (and still is for that matter), and when she is bored, which is most of the time, spends her day leaping against the sides of her kennel, bumping against the walls with the regular dull thumping, monotonous beat of a steam hammer. It is a habit which annoys the rest of the dogs, as it annoys me. Fortunately it annoyed Mrs Latham who insisted the youngster returned the bitch after the first sleepless night in the Latham household, and the next day young Colin Latham brought the bitch back on a lead, rather tearfully, walking the four miles from Lichfield to return her. It is fortunate that he did so for without her I should never have taken the incredible haul of rats from David's place; and besides, Omega, like all hyperactive dogs, would have made a lousy pet, and probably finished up biting people and killing cats.

She was four months old when I gave her away (and only a day older when young Latham returned her) and hardly an attractive dog. Her legs looked like stilts supporting a rather frail rubbery body, and her tiny head was out of place atop the compendium of legs and torso. She looked vaguely as if some genetic prankster or a divine jigsaw specialist had put together a whippet and a terrier, jumbling the parts about a bit and assembling them in haste. Later, when Alan Thomas showed her, she was to win best Jack Russell bitch at the Jack Russell Club of Great Britain—a bit of a dubious distinction considering the state of the club at that time, but as a puppy she would have taken a prize in the comical dog competition for 'The puppy I would least like to take home' class. I confess that I never really fancied her, and neither did any of my friends except Mo, who has a good eye for a dog, even a dog in an embryonic state, and Terry Rivers who helped me at pack exercise time. Only her sharp, dark quicksilver eyes, eyes which

Omega aged six weeks.

missed nothing and took in the whole of the scene at a glance, gave any indication of the bitch she would eventually become.

At that time my best rat dog was Vampire, a great hunter, a crack catch dog, but he had problems. If he was on form and relatively unruffled or upset by the day's activities, he was superb, ratting, hunting, chopping against the very feet of rival males, even mortal enemies or most mortal enemies (Warlock drove him nuts), ignoring all and sundry in his efforts to catch rats. If something had disturbed him, and it took very little to disturb him, he would leap out of the trailer and set about the nearest male or female in sight. He half-throttled two of Alan Thomas's Lakeland terriers during a particularly bad hunt, and set about a collie which had the temerity to creep up and innocently investigate the carnage of the rat hunt. Vampire saw him, whipped himself to a frenzy and attacked, screaming like a fiend. It was impossible to hunt him with Warlock, for an implacable hatred had developed between the two, a furious, blind, unreasoning hatred that set both terriers drooling white froth when they so much as saw each other. Yet Vampire was a great rat killer, heedless of pain, game to the point of near insanity, and at that time killing with a quick flick and leaving his rats. Now, as I write, he is senile, grey muzzled with runny myopic eyes, content with carrying around his rat defiantly, showing it to the rest of the pack, coming up to me every few minutes or so for praise, but during his fifth year—the time when a rat-killing dog is at his best—there were few dogs in the country to better him at rat catching. This I know to be a fact for at that time I visited

Vampire carrying a long dead rat; the mark of a senile hunter, I'm sad to say.

quite a few shows and came in contact with a hundred or so macho terrier men, all little boys at heart, all eager to prove the worth of their wards or maybe just to bolster their own egos, I really don't know. All would challenge, and most I'd try to ignore. Some would challenge so frequently or so publicly, I'd be forced into accepting the wager just to save face—then after they had made their point that they were really men with a capital 'M', they would disappear never to be seen again. John Kellogg was a different matter, however, and there was something about his quiet unassuming demeanour which made me uncertain of the outcome of the contest with him.

Like me, Kellogg was an inveterate rat hunter—to the uninitiated, rats are not regarded as suitable quarry by terrier Men, again with a capital 'M', who wear hob-nailed boots, sport suitable masculine tattoos and curiously rather feminine earrings and who tramp around the countryside for days, ostensibly to hunt a badger, but supposedly disdain rat hunting. Yet rats in number are fearsome quarry, and old rat pit dog breeders (see my book *Tales of a Rat Hunting Man*—a free plug for a book if ever there was one), used only the toughest bull terrier-blooded dogs to mate to their terriers to breed, to compete in the rat-killing spectacles involving a hundred or even a thousand rats. A dog required to hunt up and often winkle out rats from under sacks, clods of earth or rubble will usually take fearsome hidings if there are rats in number. As I write, Vampire and Pagan—reluctant kennel mates, as neither like each other very much—are so badly bitten that neither can see properly. Pagan in particular looks quite dreadful. Thus I am always puzzled by the man who digs one illegal badger a year, and gains masculinity in his own eyes for the enterprise, yet sneers at rat hunting as a sport.

Kellogg, as I've said, was different. He was a quiet, well-spoken chap of maybe the same age as I am, who was, to use his own words a self-employed painter and decorator, out of work at the moment, which is someone's loss, believe me! Kellogg never considered himself as a terrier man, as although he went out with his local hunt now and again, and his terriers acquitted themselves well on those days; most of his sport consisted of ratting along dykes and canals, a difficult sport as rats, when pushed, take to water as freely as otters, and it takes a dog and a half to catch rats in such places, particularly in mucky, rubbish-filled brooks. What was even worse, I liked Kellogg and had no reason to compete against his terriers, yet a macho crowd of half-wits somehow pushed John into a contest and before you could say

Jack Ivester Lloyd, there was five hundred pounds riding on Kellogg's two terriers against Vampire, playing on my pitch, a farm which Vampire had worked almost daily for four and a half years. Kellogg, a quiet unassuming man didn't seem particularly worried about the outcome of the event. As he explained, 'It isn't my money, Bri, and I'd love to come up for the evening anyway.'

Kellogg had four or maybe five border terriers bred down from that grand old man of border terriers, Deerstone Destiny. I'd trained and worked eight or nine of Destiny's progeny and I rated them highly, but it wasn't the breeding of the terriers which bothered me. I'd come to know Kellogg quite well over the three months which separated the challenge from the contest and watched two of his bitches working a canal with John. He was completely in tune with his team, aware of their strengths, their weaknesses, and all three seemed to be knitted into a very complete team, the sort of relationship primitive man must have had with his dogs. His dogs hunted quickly, quietly and efficiently, with the minimum of shouting and advice from John and the minimum of barking, whining and ostentation from his dogs. His hauls were small by our standards. If he took some rats on a day's outing, he went home, pleased as punch and phoned me to tell me of his triumph. In fact I felt rather badly about having him up to compete against my team during the October run, but John scarcely knew his backers; they'd heard of him, seen him at a show near Stowe, fancied their chances of taking me down a peg or so, but hadn't got dogs good enough to attempt the task themselves and had somehow pushed poor John into the contest. Normally I detest the people who challenge me; the pair of idiots who threw out a thousand pound challenge at Lambourn in 1981, shouting loudly, attracting a crowd by their jibes and running cant slang made me vomit—and these were particularly annoying because they made themselves scarce as soon as I accepted their challenge and CTF Ltd, a field sports supplier, made the challenge public.

To play a rat hunter on his own pitch is madness. Firstly, I've never been successful ratting any farm on my first visit to the place. I'd lift bins, rubbish sacks while the dogs waited eagerly for the rats to bolt. The rats would oblige of course, but promptly disappear down holes only a few feet from the piles where they were hiding. Ratting such places takes weeks for dogs and men to understand the flight paths and bolt holes of rats; and often as not, the owner of the farm who believes he is inviting the Pied Piper plus his team of terriers is so dismayed by our lack of initial success that he rarely invites us back again and simply resorts to poisoning his rats, which to tell the truth is the only really efficient way of controlling the rodents. On the farm we were to 'field' for the contest, Vampire was very much at home. He was never a particularly intelligent dog, but rats run the same paths if they possibly can, escaping along the same routes, slipping into the same holes, and all I had to do was to restrain the old devil while I blocked the exits in the dark, and Vampire did the rest. We'd played the damn game four nights a week for four years and if Vampire didn't know the place now, he never would, of that I was certain.

You know I really do sell Vampire short in this chapter. He's senile now, doddery in fact, getting involved in fights with younger dogs who will almost certainly kill him one day, but as a young dog he really was a superb worker. His nose rarely made a mistake—true, he wasn't as gifted at marking as Beltane (I've never seen a dog that was)—but he wasn't too far down the line when prizes for seeking ability were being given. I doubt whether he was ever as quick as his daughter Omega. I've never owned a dog which was, for that matter, nor could he chop at the incredible angles Pagan manages, but as an all-round rat dog he took some beating. He could anticipate, winkle out rats from crevices without the slightest regard for pain, mark through mounds of the most foetid mess which would corrode the scenting organs of a beagle or a hyena, but above all he tried harder than any terrier I've ever seen. He would work until he dropped, suffer the most frightful lacerations without complaint and still be hunting long after exhaustion had sapped his strength. His courage is still a legend, and it was his courage that damned night caused his destruction.

I live near Whittington, a small, but sadly evergrowing village which acts as a dormitory town for Birmingham, and each morning I watch the procession of young, up-and-coming executives who pour like lemmings en route for Birmingham. Within a year or two no doubt, most will have been promoted and will have forsaken their all mod. cons. neat little semis for a bigger, ritzier place nearer to Birmingham. They are temporary dwellers and cause no nuisance in the district, but a far more ephemeral dweller, a type which really gets everyone's back up is the 'to hell with it all' self-sufficiency freak who leaves his none-too-safe advertising job and prompted by a few episodes of 'The Good Life', which isn't exactly an accurate representation of country life, comes out to my neck of the woods to 'rough it'. Roughing it however, means generally fooling about, making a temporary ripple in the big pool called the countryside before becoming thoroughly disenchanted by the rustic life and hightailing it back to Birmingham once more. Each year I watch them settle in the nearby rented cottages, mostly trendy, thirty year olds, with beards and lumberjack jackets, but the first frosts of winter sees them off. Early autumn will find them picking elderberries to make wine and browsing through the beds of feral comfrey at the end of the lane. Spurred on no doubt by the initial success of the fermenting wine, they will race hot foot to Penkridge market to buy a trio of totally unsuitable Muscovy ducks and a few knackered out fancy bantams. A rabbit or so from some commercial (though the word commercial is a bit questionable regarding rabbits nowadays) herd will usually complete the *tout ensemble* and in no time at all we are clear of Keats 'Autumn' and into a very sticky and unpleasant winter. The winters around here are hard and usually see off most of the trendies. A few more hardy members may even take two years of battering, fortified by donations from rich daddies who hope to God their erring kids will see the light, or by taking on temporary commissions, prostituting their 'Good Life' image a little perhaps, but what the hell, they've tried, haven't they? Self-sufficiency is hell, and in a tiny cottage with a small plot of land is only possible if one is capable of working say fifty hours a day. As I've said, most leave quickly enough and after a while a brand new batch of weirdos appear down at my shack, learning snaring and other skills which in a year or so they will use to regale and fascinate their half-drunken clients as they wine and dine at some smart Midland restaurant, no doubt relating how they met this incredible rustic who kept terriers, lurchers and a mess of ferrets. Oh, why the hell do I knock them? I went through the same growing-up process and perhaps didn't learn as quickly as they will. On the subject of lurchers—don't worry, I'll be back to the main theme presently—most of these self-sufficiency freaks keep the most outlandish dogs as companions, rather than an honest-to-goodness collie lurcher which would suit well around here. The present crop, a young buck with his red-headed wife, own an Alaskan Mulemute, a hairy sled dog from the Yukon, which might be a joy if their car breaks down mid-winter, but is a dead loss as regards hunting up edible quarry, but the one I'll always remember is the Giant Schnauzer—not because I like Giant Schnauzers (I don't: I've even had to look up how to spell Schnauzer) but because one damn nigh did me out of £500, and hey-ho, as promised we're back to the main theme once again, and as Rapunzel said to the Silver Prince of

Laguna—'about bloody time, mate, about bloody time'.

I exercise Vampire alone or with Pagan, as firstly, he doesn't pack well even with bitches and secondly, he is hell let loose with dogs. Terrier males irritate him and all of my studs quite simply leave him alone. Large dogs drive him to paroxysms of rage, and 'there's the rub'. Disregard the humbug about a good little'un beating a good big'un, because it just isn't true of dogs or of men. Charlie Magri would not only be defeated by Larry Holmes, in all probability he would be killed. Likewise, a small dog, however aggressive he might be, would come to grief against a bigger dog. I once witnessed my uncle, an unpleasant reprobate by some standards, but totally fascinating to me, bet a large border collie against a thirty pound, half-bred bull terrier and clean up fifty-five pounds from the bewildered miners he so regularly milked. Hence, unless Vampire's initial fury puts a bigger dog to flight, and it invariably does, the old devil is on to a hiding to nothing if he comes to terms with a dog four times his weight.

Well the night in question, I was exercising Vampire alone across the fields, weaving a careful way between two bulls tethered in the twenty-five acre—supposedly breeding bulls, but they act as the finest poaching deterrent imaginable. We turned the hawthorn hedge, a decaying broken affair and chanced on the self-sufficiency buff exercising his Giant Schnauzer. I saw them and reached down to grasp Vampire, but Vampire had seen them first. He bristled, and a low moan rather than a snarl escaped from his throat as he exploded and flew at the huge dog. Perhaps generations of show breeding have dulled the edge of this once useful dog or maybe Schnauzers, despite their terrier shape, were never designed to be aggressive. There was little time to reflect on the evolution of this large grey dog, however, for with a resounding smack Vampire had careered into the poor unsuspecting devil, some sixty odd pounds was bowled over by the fury of Vampire's attack. It looked incongruous, this twelve pound fiend bowling over this hairy grey giant, and for a moment, as the Schnauzer attempted to get the hell out of the place, I questioned Uncle Billy's wisdom as to whether a good big'un will always defeat a little'un, but secretly I knew that there could be only one outcome to such a fight and raced in to stop it, while the self-sufficiency man squeezed himself tightly against the hedge to avoid contact with the grapplers. I saw the huge grey dog strike rapidly at Vampire, more in desperation than aggression, the head darting out like a cobra, a head almost as big as Vampire's entire body. It couldn't have been more than a ten second battle between the time Vampire made contact with the beast to the time I dragged the screaming and roaring Vampire off the dog, carefully preventing the now battle-mad terriers striking at my hands, and shouting a quick apology at the self-sufficiency buff, I carried Vampire home, while he wriggled and writhed, roaring to be back at the German dog. I breathed a sigh of relief, no harm had been done, no wounds were visible on the old devil and I doubt if he'd had time to come to terms with the bigger dog, time enough that is to commit any damage. However, as usual I was wrong about the outcome of the fight. Those two darting strikes from the Schnauzer had gone home leaving two deep punctures in Vampire's face—one either side of his muzzle, narrowly missing his eyes and probably puncturing the fine bone tissue which leads off from the honeycombed muzzle. The result was that Vampire's face swelled to bull terrier proportions, one eye closing completely. Things couldn't have been worse. In two weeks time I was due to play Kellogg and the £500 my backers had put up looked very much like being poured down the drain.

It never rains but it pours, could be the motto of the Plummer coat of arms (two hypochondriacs rampant over a copy of *Das Kapital*) and for the next seven or eight days it was one thing after another going wrong. Name it, and it went wrong; sometimes, I confess, through mismanagement, but mostly through bad luck. Things were bad in school, which I confess is nothing new, while bitch after bitch went down with something or other. Set, who had had a litter of six superb puppies sired by Laddie, collapsed with hypocalcaemia (humans call it milk fever!) and promptly expired as soon as the vet put the needle in her vein to pump in a curious sounding canine panacea called calcium boroglutinate. Normally this brings a bitch out of a milk fever fit in seconds, but in Set's case it didn't work for she died with her teeth still snapping at the needle. Beltane, Vampire's sister whelped a litter of puppies to Eric Taylor's dog, or rather tried to whelp a litter, for she 'jammed' while I was at school and I returned home to find a very desperate bitch with a huge puppy just about ready to come into the world but jammed in the breach. The bitch must have been like that for maybe two or three hours and uterine inertia, literally a tired womb, had just about guaranteed that a Caesarian section would be necessary. All in all things were looking quite desperate and I began to wonder how I could wriggle out of the bet and still save face.

It was difficult, make no bones about it. Accepting the bet was a mistake, not because Vampire couldn't cope with Kellogg's bitches,

I'm sure he could, if he was 'right' that is, but simply because by accepting the wager I practically gave licence for the most amazing band of weirdos to visit my house. 'Are yer breeding 'em,' sneered Mo, glancing at a pair of tattooed lunatics, one whose neck sported a malformed serpent devouring a pot bellied swan, who materialised uninvited and certainly unwelcomed to inspect my dogs (Kellogg phoned that evening to say he was getting the same treatment from his backers but it didn't trouble me much, I'm afraid). Daily, crowds of inarticulate lunatics seem to spring from nowhere with insufficient money to tax their vans, but, seemingly with enough to put £500 on a rat killing contest. They eyed up my rather scruffy cottage, sneered at my lack of furnishings, were very critical of my dogs, stating that Charlie Crutchley, an irritating chap with an equally unlikely name, had terriers which could whip the hides off all my dogs, outstayed their welcome from the moment they arrived and finally cleaned out their mucky vans, dumping their rubbish on the piece of land just outside my cottage. One lout, a star on each ear, really enjoyed himself at my place I'm sure for he lamented the fact that he had no transport of his own, for if he had, he said he'd spend most of his time at my place. They were a dreadful bunch, unpleasant to look at, smelly and boring as a wart. I'm not bright, gifted or able to do anything in any way other than my ability to catch rats by hand. I can also wiggle both ears independently, and then there isn't all that much call for that sort of stuff is there, but people who fail to make any sort of reasonable conversation bore the pants off me—and I'd have put that a bit stronger if this wasn't in print.

Supposedly human speech developed because of man's hunting abilities. While he was swinging through the trees munching bananas, or whatever man's arboreal ancestors munched, man needed little in the way of vocabulary—come to think of it, there's not much that one could class as scintillating that can be said about bananas—but as soon as his foot hit the deck and he took up hunting instead of munching fruits, man developed an extensive vocabulary. At least that's what Ardrey says, and far be it for anyone to argue with Ardrey. Thus it could be said that man's hunting instinct helped in producing an extensive vocabulary. Things ain't what they used to be, mate—leastways, not if one studied the set which invaded my cottage during the three weeks prior to my contest. All wore hobnailed boots, most were tattooed, a few had earrings (and oh God, how I hate bloody earrings on a man) and all found the process of speech a bit taxing, to

Kellogg's Border terrier.

say the least; but to cut a long story short I decided Vampire was *hors de combat* and made up my mind to pull a ringer and use Battle for the contest. I keep a strain, a bunch of suicidal spiteful lookalikes, but a strain nevertheless, and lookalikes certainly, and thus to substitute Battle (Vampire's daughter) for Vampire was child's play. A few might just notice that Battle didn't have a penis, but I guessed few of the group would be articulate enough to express their suspicion. Battle was a good rat killer, about number four in the pack and had ratted the farm so often that I had no doubt she could handle Kellogg's border terriers. She was quick, efficient, keen to get rid of her rat as soon as she had bitten it, and this makes for a top-grade rat hunting dog; and while she lacked Vampire's thrust I was fairly certain that she was as fast a rat killer as I could produce on the night. That is, until the day the stoats moved into the hedgerow just opposite my dog run. Cue for another chapter and if I haven't lost the reader in my splurge about Ardrey, I can promise the rest of the book gets quite interesting.

Incidentally I've just watched a video of a TV interview I did last year. I move both ears independently even when I'm not trying: boy, that's a habit I really must get out of—and quick. Now read on.

The Stoats

There have always been stoats in my lane, at least for the fifteen years since I've lived here; and scarcely a morning goes by without one scuttling out from under as I start up my battered and noisy car. Mo thinks it's the rats which seem to be omnipotent guests in my hedgerow that bring the stoats; but it's the rabbits on Cope and Barlow's land that ensures the stoat population stays high. Even as I write this chapter with winter fast on the horizon, the night resounds with high-pitched yickers and screams which tell that the stoats are hunting and somewhere out there in the blackness under some hedge or along the edges of the brooks which criss-cross the countryside around my cottage, a fearsome struggle is taking place.

All in all, I suppose I really like stoats. At one time when I bred and reluctantly reared game fowl for Bill Petheridge, a one hundred per cent idiot who with twice as much brain as he now possesses would still be a half-wit, I cursed the stoats which took the occasional game chick or so when the hens sat clutches under my hawthorn hedge: Petheridge, that's going back a bit—a man with a whim and an idea and nothing else to back it. Petheridge was an 'expert' on country matters, full of fast buck ideas which involved someone who had a modest acreage of land and no money to stock it. I met him at Lichfield small livestock market where Mo was trying to con a nest of young ferrets from a belligerent teenager, knowledgeable as only the very young seem to be. Petheridge lived in a council house but had big ideas and because I am too weak-willed to resist, my place became the resting place of a dozen or so young duckling gamefowl, fowl which strayed on the road, caused havoc in Gerald's wheat field, foraged as best they could, after which I had to buy wheat to feed them while Petheridge occasionally deigned to supervise the venture, and sometimes—more than just occasionally—bringing a really villainous disreputable or so up to see the stock. Finally the disreputables, aided and abetted by the stoats, whittled down Petheridge's game fowl to nil and I didn't see him until just last week when he materialised with another world-beating scheme for rearing a litter of unregistered greyhound whelps on my premises (my expense, my kennels, my labour, his enjoyment). I refused categorically of course. 'The place would be alive with bloody tinkers,' I mumbled. 'They've got Volvos and Mercs,' protested Petheridge, whose only criteria of anyone worthwhile is that they should own a Volvo or a Merc. 'It'll be your fault that I have to put the litter down,' he roared accusingly as he drove off in his 'L' registration Merc. As I said, I like stoats; they saw off some of Petheridge's stock and prevented him from coming up here, so I've cause to be grateful to the entire species, I suppose.

I've hunted stoats; in fact it's a novelty when my pack don't run one while out at exercise, the pack baying like thunder, the stoat spitting like fury, leaving the air drenched with its strong wild smell before it disappears down some impossibly small mousehole in the hedgerow adjoining the grove, leaving me standing there amazed that such a large animal should pour into such a tiny hole. I drive past the grove on my way to work and wind down the window to inhale that strange pungent smell, a scent which lingers around the grove for days after one of the very rare successful hunts and causes the dogs to stink for a month or two afterwards.

I bombed and gassed the hedgerow.

Stoats provided great sport, and, pre-myxomatosis, few terrier men didn't encourage their terriers to try for a tilt or so at this quicksilver little beast. Gladdish Hulkes, a curious man, who on his death-bed willed his entire Sealyham pack to Lucas, hunted a pack of terriers to stoat in the New Forest. Lucas had terrific respect for this incredibly articulate old man who had amassed a set of stories concerning the New Forest which should have been recorded for posterity. As it was, no-one thought it fit to record the old man's memories and he passed into history seemingly distinguished only by the fact that he kept a pack of Sealyhams to hunt stoat. On my death, will my only claim to fame be, that I kept a pack of terriers to hunt rat? Well, perhaps it won't make such a bad epitaph, I suppose.

I kept ducks at the time of the contest with Kellogg—not because I like ducks (I don't), but because I had this absurd self-sufficiency hang up and ducks lay an egg a day for the whole of their paranoid, noisy, smelly life, and only those who have kept ducks in a confined space know how they stink. They weren't a success with me, however; maybe because I'm just not duck minded, for all they did was to trample down their weed-filled run and turn the whole patch into a slimy, sticky quagmire, a quagmire which literally shimmered with an oily iridescence during the wet weather and stank like a Middle Eastern toilet during the warm spells. Perhaps they did lay an egg a day, they may have done for all I know; but instead of laying in their sweet-smelling straw-filled nest boxes like decent self-respecting hens, they simply dropped their eggs in the horrid stinking goo of the run, and if I wanted the eggs I had to paddle around in the filth, feeling for them, looking like an extra from that Silvano Mangano film *Bitter Rice*. No indeed, the ducks weren't a success, except with the rats, that is.

I've always had rats down the lower run. They were here when I came fifteen years ago, eking out a precarious existence among the scrap iron which littered my garden and no doubt they will be here when I've gone. Rats are creatures of habit, and once they have colonised an area they take some shifting. You can poison a colony, gas them until not even a single youngster remains and a month later some stray doe will find her way to your premises, smell the 'slick' (that curious greasy musk laid down by passing rats) around the edges of the warren, and in no time flat you are back in the rat-breeding business again. I've just poisoned a thieving little colony in my roof, a merry band which scraped away the concrete at the gable end and ran riot among the rafters, coming on top form and seemingly in party mood about midnight, and racing around, living it up until dawn. They're dead now, victims of one of those poisons which makes them weaker and weaker until they finally totter into death—humane poisons, I think they're called. Effective poisons they are however, but within a month another little wanderer will scale my hawthorn bush and gnaw out the concrete and once again trip the light fantastic on my bedroom ceiling. Normally rats don't cause much trouble; my dogs are all inoculated and I don't normally feed meal. After dusk they disturb the dogs, which go frantic to get out of their runs to get the rats scurrying about in the darkness, but if I tell the truth, my ever-present rat colony causes little harm. When I had the ducks, however, it was a different matter.

Rats like ducks, or maybe they simply hate ducks, I'm not certain. All I know is that to rear ducks from a day old to some five or six weeks requires a rat-proof pen and, brother, if you think you've got a rat-proof pen, think again. A small gap is enough to let a rat in a small slit in the flooring; enough to allow him a start to burrow, scratch and gnaw his way in, and once he does, believe me, you are in business. A rat hell-bent on getting into a duck pen really does cause havoc. Rats set about ducklings with a gusto which puts Vincent Price on the rampage, to shame. Choice morsels are eaten off still-living victims and the pitiful quackings and flutterings simply drive the ecstatic rats to greater efforts. My own pen was not rat-proof, few of my pieces of carpentry look anything less than slap-happy; so most mornings would find some very dead and very mutilated ducklings on the straw. It would take a very peculiar type of man not to react to the sights which greeted me each morning and I swore death to each and every rat for miles around. I poured petrol down every rat hole along the hedge, put heavy bricks across the mouth of each hole and fired the lot, feeling a warm glow of satisfaction at the muffled thuds below my feet, knowing that the rats' nests, kits, fleas, the lot would be cremated by the withering heat in the warren. Rats will argue with the ferrets, and even drive one from a warren, but there is no answer to the flash, the explosion and the blistering heat which follows a petrol attack on a warren. I suppose it's illegal, and damnably illegal at that, and it's most certainly inhuman, but the sight of those lacerated ducklings would drive St Francis to similar atrocities, believe me. I bombed the entire hedgerow that morning, but the following day saw further deaths amongst the ducklings. I turned Beltane loose at night, an action which saw off a few of the devils, but each morning I would take

Battle and Omega along the roadside while a friend rattled the sheds and hedgerows with a stick, pushing any skulking rat out to the pair.

Berry hunted with me in those days. It's easy to get a ratting team for a spectacular night's hunting at the poultry farm, when TV cameras, radio recorders or glamorous TV stars are present, but it requires a very special sort of person to get up at six to assist in what often turns out to be an abortive and often fruitless expedition. Berry was such a person. He was old—God knows how old, a man ceases to age after his sixty-fifth birthday as far as I'm concerned—and irritating with it. It's perhaps a right that old men have (together with a pension) to rabbit on about things long gone, exaggerating, glorifying the old days and generally annoying all and sundry with their bygones. Still, I miss Berry these days, his silly talk of pre-war bacon and its flavour which was somehow lost as soon as the first shot was fired in anger, in the days when men were really men and Unisex only a hideous dream. At first he drove me nuts, particularly after his wife died and he came up to my place maybe five or six times a day, using any pretext to break the awful loneliness and monotony of his now very empty life. He'd worked on the railways for maybe fifty years and probably had loads of really good tales to tell, yet he never got round to telling them. In fact the only thing that sticks in my mind about Berry was that he was a wart-buyer—I'll explain.

Warts are curious things and there doesn't seem to be a lot men know about them. They come and go as their fancies take them, or perhaps as their owner's fancies take them, for there's a lot to suggest that warts will go if their owners want them to go. When I was a kid my hands were speckled with the ugly things, great blackened blobs which defied the attentions of my mother, dabbing them with an irritating solution of silver nitrate. The corrosive chemical simply burned them, making them blacker still and even more unsightly. Then, one morning, when I woke up, they'd gone, every last grotty one of them. Warts are like that. One of my friends, also afflicted with warts, rubbed them with a piece of raw liver ('got to be stolen liver,' says Mo, all Mo's gypsy remedies seem to require stolen meat or stolen anything for that matter), buried the liver in the garden and as the liver rotted so did the warts. The process is called sympathetic magic in the mumbo jumbo world of witchcraft. The trouble is such a process is often as effective as modern medicine in the treatment of warts; and most medical schools refuse to treat warts, as they know that the folk medicine cures work just as well and often a damn sight

Berry and I.

better. Berry simply bought his warts.

A child with a particularly nasty wart would be brought to Berry who, like a property surveyor, would assess the value of the said wart and pay the child for it, uttering such rubbish as 'I'll buy that wart for 10p,' or if it was a particularly good wart, not that I'm an expert on what constitutes a first class wart mind you, maybe 20p. The kid would be encouraged to spend his or her ill gotten gains from his wart sales, and true to form the wart, now no longer owned by the child would vanish. Crazy, yes, I thought so, but it worked, believe me, I've seen it; for there's a whole lot of juju practised in the isolated areas between the dormitory towns. Child would get up one morning to note the wart had somehow vanished leaving a patch of very normal if slightly pink skin where a black filthy wart once sat. I used to laugh at such hocus-pocus once, but I've been fifteen years in this curious district and I no longer doubt the power of suggestion among country folk. All in all, it's only in the last few hundred years that country folk ceased to believe in the basilisk, a creature with a cock's head, and a serpent's claws whose glance was fatal. (I worked for such a creature once in a school in Rotherham.)

Berry suffered from an irritating malaise that smites down the very old and the teenager for Berry, like all geriatrics and macho boys 'knew it all'. He ridiculed my theories of entering terriers, knocked my methods of detecting the first stages of milk fever and became what Moses describes as a regular 'pain in the arse'. But he was one of the few who stuck with me, exercising the dogs at dawn with me, and though he complained bitterly about the icy morning chill which bit into his bones, his awful loneliness would ensure he'd be making tea while I hurriedly dressed to get Battle fit for the Kellogg contest. It's funny that, but as I write I can still hear his mumblings from my untidy kitchen even though he died of a stroke five years ago. ('Should have sold it to someone,' sneered Mo unkindly.)

The morning in question was just like any other I suppose, with Battle and the juvenile Omega hunting together—well, Battle hunting and Omega watching, for Omega had never quite learned the knack of hunting. Battle had run a rat that morning, pushing it under the duck pen where it hissed and spat at the stick I was using to drive it out. It was an old doe and as it bolted, slipping past Battle to die with a deft flick from Omega, I fondly hoped it had been the fiend which had attacked and eaten alive the ducklings. So preoccupied was I with dealing out vengeance to the old doe that I was unaware of the deadly precision of Omega's thrust, the shake that neatly severed the spine before sending the cadaver spinning across the ground. She had killed rats before, a hundred maybe or two hundred on David's farm, joining in each worry, becoming as amorphous as the rest of the dogs during a scrimmage, but today she had finally chosen to awaken from obscurity. It's the same with fighters, boxers or maybe even wrestlers. One day, for some unknown reason, they hit form and, bingo! they become world beaters; however, so elated was I with the death of what I considered to be the old villainess who had slain my ducks, that I scarcely noticed that Omega and not Battle had brought about the rat's demise. An hour later however I was to have no doubt that Omega had finally become the exquisite connoisseur of death I know her to be.

I threw the scaly old doe to my ferrets, and mindful of the havoc I assumed she had wrought on the ducklings, I watched gleefully as the ferrets munched into the old devil, seemingly oblivious of her obvious senility, and that the flesh of the old harridan must have been as tough as leather. 'There's summat wrong with people who get pleasure watching beasts being torn up by ferrets,' whittered Old Berry, peering into the cage himself, reluctant to miss one moment of the gory

Feeding dead rats to ferrets.

feast. 'Summat wrong,' he repeated, staring hard at me as he did.

We walked up from the bottom run to put the dogs away while I went into a state of deep melancholy about the forthcoming day at school. 'Old Mr Batterby could 'ave tamed 'em,' (Berry was always complaining about the way 'us youngsters coped with the kids')

Omega demonstrates her superiority over the Border terrier.

whined Berry. 'Mr Batterby could, by God he could. Tamed us he did, right scared of him we wus.' Mr Batterby taught fourteen year old, respectful white lads. I taught sixteen-year-old disruptives who would have butchered, bled and bagged up Mr Batterby before he could have opened up his cane cupboard and extracted his No. 7 Stinger. It was useless to tell Berry this, for Berry had Old Man's disease and knew it all. He was about to repeat the tale of how Mr Batterby managed to detect and tame the phantom turnip thief (big deal, Batterby, big deal) when a stoat exploded from the cover and shot across the road in front of Battle. I saw her lunge, chop and flick and the air became filled with the pungent scent of the mustelid. She shook her head sharply and only then did I realise that quick as she was the stoat had put in four good bites before she sent it rolling across the gravel. I held up the body of the stoat gingerly but with pride. 'What do you think of this, Berry, I'll tell you Kellogg hasn't got a bloody chance,' but Berry wasn't listening. Omega stood by his feet shaking her head to ease a set of stinging, smarting bites on her muzzle. In the road lay the bodies of three large yearling stoats, necks at a curiously jaunty angle, which had broken cover at the same time as Battle's victim. Even Berry, who underrates my triumphs, was elated at the speed of Omega's lunges. 'Never seen owt like it,' he whispered. 'Like a bloody flash, excepting me Dad's collie Rover,' he added, and with false teeth clicking inanely he imitated Omega's lightning flicks. School passed joyously that day and well before 11 a.m. I had decided to use Omega as a ringer for Vampire.

She annihilated Kellogg's team so decisively that even his backers didn't ask for a rematch. A few sneered, 'Is she owt good for fox?' but they realised I'd never use her on fox as long as she lived. It would be a bit like using a rapier to chop wood. So spectacular was her prowess that night that no-one noticed the 'switch', though to the end of the evening Kellogg did nudge me and whisper, 'Curious that, Bri, I always thought Vampire was a dog!'

The Trailer

Now I'll make no bones about it, next to taking up teaching as a career, or reversing into Janos Grabotsky's Rolls Royce, the biggest mistake I've ever made in my life was inviting, correction, allowing, Caroline to come and live with me. Not only were we worlds apart socially (her father was a retired general and a major stockholder in a major company or other, whereas in my family we regard anyone with a birth certificate as being a bit toffee-nosed) but I am quite simply a confirmed bachelor, a decided individualist, or, as Moses puts it most eloquently, 'the most selfish bastard in the world'.

Perhaps it was her posh accent that attracted me or maybe the fact that I'd never met anyone with a double-barrelled name before, but whatever it was, her coming to live at my cottage was the biggest mistake ever. Oh, she was glamorous all right, and I mean glamorous, for she worked as a model for *Vogue* or some other magazine that one finds on a dentist's waiting room table. Winch of the Fell and Moorland met her once and said 'Bri, where do you get 'em?' a comment I treated as an appreciation of my taste in women, but on reflection he could have been enquiring where such women hang out so that he could avoid going to such places, but perhaps I'm being unkind. No, hell, I'm not being unkind, Caroline was, in addition to being a snotty-nosed little thing, the biggest bore in the world, as predictable as a slice of Battenburg cake with a set of six or seven clichés she repeated over and over again. For instance, cliché one, prefixed by a simpering little grin, was 'I wouldn't mind being on the shelf providing I was taken down and dusted now and again'—a saying she repeated so often during her stay that the total would have looked like a space-invaders score. God, she was boring, and it is rumoured that men trapped in her company at parties have been known to bite off their legs to escape. My handwriting has just taken a sudden wobble due to a shudder induced by the memory of her.

She was my first contact with the upper class—and my last, I expect, for I learned to know my station in life after meeting her. Dad with his communism—and he was such a rampant communist that it is rumoured that Karl Marx and Lenin avoided him on the street out of principle—would have hated Caroline as he hated all the upper class; but, truth be told, the nearest he ever got to an aristocrat was the manager of the local Co-op. Whereas I treated Dad as a one hundred per cent Bolshevik lunatic, after meeting Caroline I realised Dad may have had something about the upper class—that's if Caroline was anything to go by.

It's curious but I can't remember where or when I met Caroline, let alone how I somehow invited her to move in. The mind is that sort of machine, I guess, and it blots out all the unpleasant events and only allows a person to remember the good times. Thus there is little I can remember about National Service, teacher training or the dreaded reign of Caroline Woods-Godfrey, though I'll say one thing for the upper class, they are born stickers, game to the bloody last for when she moved in there was no way I could get her to go. I firmly believe that if the Woods-Godfreys had been Viceroys, we would have still had India for once a Woods-Godfrey moved in there was no shifting one.

I knew from the day she came we were unsuited—and boy, do I mean unsuited!—for each other. I've never been one for creature comforts—in fact it's only in the last five years that I've bothered to own my own knife and fork. So her first question, 'Did I own an automatic dishwasher?' really threw me. 'Yeh,' replied Moses, quick as a flash, 'she's called Fathom,' and he glanced down at the lurcher at my feet. Caroline froze slightly, twisted her lips in a somewhat disgusted fashion and managed to give Moses a pitying look and me a hostile stare at the same time. Round one to Caroline; and from then on I never gained a points superiority. Moses slunk away and rarely came to the house from then on, and my friends became fewer and fewer driven away by snide little comments about people who are work-shy, stupid, and nasty little digs about smells, comments about which my nearest and dearest are decidedly (though I must add deservedly) touchy. One by one they slunk off, driven away by Caroline's snooty attitude and sneering glances.

Hell, I tried to get rid of her—and believe me no-one tried harder! I began by pointing out that I wasn't really good enough for her (a point about which she agreed wholeheartedly) going on to suggest that she found someone more of her class to even shouting down a paper megaphone, 'Go home, you bitch, I hate you,' but Caroline—Caroline was staying put and her reply was always a little sneery smile and a half-lisped, 'But this is my home now.' Finally I had to assert myself and did the only manly thing I could think of. I built a wall across the middle of the house and moved in next door, so to speak. 'Taking the his and her bit a little far, laddie,' said Arthur Templer, an out-of-work actor of the type that went out of fashion with Beerbohm Tree, but I had to do it just to get away from the awful boredom that was rotting my mind and the constant day in, day out, 'instant mash' that was playing hell with my hiatus hernia.

You know, living in the solitude of my side of the house, a solitude punctuated by the occasional snooty sniff from next door (Caroline never said anything, she sniffed it) my mind began to run riot, and for a short period of time I think I went stark staring nuts, for all I could think of were methods of putting an end to the snooty sniffer on the other side of the wall. I used to lie awake at night and eulogise over methods of her demise, a smile creasing my mouth as I envisaged her going through David Hancock's chicken meal grater, a powerful mincer that could render a bullock to pepper-like dust in minutes, or of dropping her into the cement mixers of the A38 by-pass, thereby enabling passing motorists to gaze in amazement as one of the pillars supporting the by-pass gave a happy family group a sneer as they drove past. At the time of writing I bet there are thousands of blokes contemplating similar fates for unwanted wives and mistresses, but it takes real guts to do it. That chap off 'Malice Aforethought' who saw off a whole load of unwanted birds deserved an OBE, not the gallows, believe me. But just as I was setting out on the search for a poison unknown to the toxicologist—imagining the Lichfield CID Inspector saying 'Damn it, Plummer, you're a clever devil, we know you've done for her, but how?'—Caroline upped and left and married the owner of a local night club. Incidentally, he has just recently opened up another club in Beirut and is living there, maybe using Beirut as a tax haven, but my own theory is that the 'instant mash' got him and he's gone there to recuperate.

She took all the furniture, mind you—well, it was hers to take anyway, and Mo who turned up the very next day said rather sagely, 'D'ye know I've never really realised how big your house is until the furniture went.' Every scrap of furniture vanished, she even took the curtains, burning them on a smouldering pile under my damson tree. Now just in case you are wondering if this is the wrong book, or maybe the book-binder has run amok and put in a chapter from an entirely different book, I'll get back to the tale proper and mention the only thing she left behind in her haste to leave 'Chez Plummers' was the trailer, a neat little four-by-three device she towed behind her souped-up sports car—a brightly varnished piece of equipment that campers tow behind the family car—not that Caroline was a camper, for the thought of the open air life would have snuffed her out.

'Stow it in the nettles, Mo,' I hissed, 'I'm going to keep this.' 'For what!' Mo said cryptically. 'I'll carry the dogs in it,' I whispered. Mo eyed its open top. 'They'll jump out,' he uttered philosophically, but he reckoned not with my natural genius and the fact that I knew one Steve Jones, a native of Burton and a wizard with metal work with skills enough to make Tubalcain look like one of those demonstrators on 'Playschool'. Within a week of Caroline's much delayed departure, Steve had constructed a superb piece of metallic engineering resembling a plated Italian World War II tank, capable of carrying twelve terriers and looking so unlike the original trailer that even Sherlock Holmes would have been thrown by the metamorphosis. It was a masterpiece of engineering and probably the toughest little trailer the world has ever seen—it had to be, and here begins the tale proper.

Not only do I use the trailer for carrying dogs, but also for transporting carcasses of fallen beasts and when my interest in gardening started up (it lasted roughly four months) for transporting sundry piles of animal yucky which would have festered its way through the lead lining of an atomic pile. And—as a final piece of advertising for Steve Jones constructions—it acted like a magnet for Rollo, Omega's son who would christen it maybe twenty times a day and, at the risk of appearing crude, Rollo's spray could turn a pair of brand new Levis or other ultimate jeans into a scene from a Walt Disney moth attack in hours. (Rollo has some fairly disgusting habits and while few of our rat team object to seeing him work, no-one will volunteer to stand next to him.) But these are small fry incidents when one considers the awful night of the 14th June.

Now I am fairly convinced that trailers are living things and not only possess life, but also a mind of their own. I know a hundred, maybe a thousand people who boast they can reverse a light trailer from some pretty sticky places, but I fail to see how in hell they can. I follow each and every instruction to the letter, even positioning the wheels of my car when parking car and trailer. But as soon as I try to turn the combination reversing the car plus trailer things go awry—no, amok is the only word for it—and my trailer can easily be followed by tracking the number of dented cars with smears of black bituminous

Rollo resistant paint found on each dent. Once while fetching a load of duck offal from Birmingham during a spell of hot weather—not a pretty sight believe me—I reversed the trailer neatly past a Jensen driven by a mini-skirted dolly bird, who smiled at my reversing aplomb, straight slam bang into the brand new Rolls Royce of Janos Grabotsky who closed his eyes in horror, murmuring a little Jewish prayer to avert the disaster perhaps. So much for Jewish prayers, for not only did my trailer crash slam bang into Grabotsky's car, but the back doors jarred by the impact swung open and disgorged about sixty pounds of rancid duck offal complete with macabre Aylesbury heads across the bonnet of his gleaming car. He stood there awhile simply staring in disbelief while I raced across, scrabbling the near luminous half-rotted offal into the trailer. 'Do you want my insurance number?' I asked timidly for Grabotsky is not only rich but enormously powerfully built. 'No,' he replied quietly in a voice totally unfitting his huge bulk. 'I simply want to die,' and tears began to roll down his cheeks. It is not a pleasant sight to see a man cry, and to see a large powerful man, a man noted for his skill with the back break, doing so, is most disconcerting, and with frantic haste I scraped off the fatty duck offal from his car bonnet while a horrified crowd gathered to watch the spectacle. 'What is it?' said an old man with a Brummy accent, 'what yer going to do with it?' 'I'm, I'm delivering it to a Chinese restaurant,' I said desperately. 'You a Riar, a damned Riar,' shouted a voice and glancing up I saw a pair of enraged Orientals working themselves into a frenzy. Now I've seen all the Bruce Lee films so rather than chance a Nagasaki nose throw or a glancing blow with a rice flail, I decided to quicken my pace, scooping the horrid goo into the trailer while Grabotsky's tears continued to roll down his huge muscular face. A child kicked a duck head in the gutter—'Is he a puppet maker, Mam, does he make puppets?' said the macabre little sod. 'Ask him, Mam, can I 'ave one Mam?' but Mum merely dragged the little ghoul into the crowd. I finished cleaning most of the guts, slime and goo off Grabotsky's car and half whispered 'I'm awfully sorry', offering my hand as a peace gesture. 'Don't touch me,' screamed Grabotsky leaping back from me lest I should besmirch his £200 suit. 'If there's anything I can do' I asked sheepishly. 'There is!' answered Grabotsky. 'Stay away from bloody Birmingham, you sodding madman!' he wailed as I drove off hurriedly, away from the disaster area.

 Now it speaks highly for both Rolls-Royce's and Steve Jones' enterprises that neither vehicle was even scratched, but that evening Rick

James, a gents' outfitters assistant with a casual if uninformed interest in dogs, visited my shack that evening. Over tea he became excited and said 'Do you know there was a bloody duck's head in the gutter in New Street today? Bloody Pakkis and their ritual killings, the buggers should be stopped!' but my mind was too filled by the vision of a ritual killing being perpetrated by one Janos Grabotsky to reply. Yet, as I've said, this is nothing compared to the incident of the dreaded 14th June.

So on with the tale without so much as a single digression. June 14th, being a Thursday, was naturally a rat hunting night for, come hell or high water, Thursday night merits a rat hunt. In fact, if given a choice between an evening with Fiona Richmond or a rat hunt, the rats would have it. (Please God do not punish me for that awful lie!) So into trailer with Omega, Battle, Vampire, Beltane, Pagan, carefully avoiding carrying Pagan with Omega for things were a little hectic at this time and that's putting it mildly. Into the car with Bob Green, a school teacher friend. 'Clip the trailer up Bob,' I shouted while parrying a lunge from Beltane at Omega—for things weren't too good there either.

Now my trailer towed behind my tiny Fiat 126 ('You're ripping the guts out of a car that size, Bri') is connected by a socket that fastens over a ball rather like my hip joint used to before my recent accident, and the whole lot—the trailer (not my hip joint)—is kept in place by a pin which passes through the joint. It does a pretty good job too, that is if the pin is in place and the person linking up the trailer knows exactly what he is doing. Tonight, however, Bob did not know exactly what he was doing and the trailer pin was not in place; and here begins the tragedy.

Mick and Rog followed behind in their van while Bob, who is braver than either, travelled with me. Burton Old Road, under the bridge, over the crossing, stop at junction, so far so good. Things however rarely run smoothly for me, and as we were entering the main road entering into Lichfield things went decidedly amiss. We entered the road and drove past a row of character-filled terraced houses. 'They'll tear these down and build characterless houses for up and coming young execs' I hissed philosophically, dwelling on my superspecial subject. Bob's face had gone white however, 'The trailer' he whispered and glancing in the driving mirror I spied the trailer going off at right angles to the car straight across the road towards the fenced in cottage gardens of the terraced houses at a rate strangely faster than the speed of the car and gathering impetus by the second. We stopped and without daring to turn, watched in the driving mirror, the trailer mount the pavement, smash through the fence and disappear from view.

The next few seconds are a blur, I'm afraid, as I raced across the road to the gap in the fence only to see the trailer plough across the garden and smash through the next fence and come to rest with a crash against the outside toilet of the next but one garden (personally, I like outside privvys—there's something character forming about them, but I digress, for this could quite easily degenerate into a book about WCs). A man hoeing a row of something or other in the first garden stood transfixed, open mouthed in horror as if he were witnessing the Russians suddenly invading Lichfield. 'I think it went through the next fence,' he managed to croak. We raced across the tyremarks where the trailer had ploughed through a neat but scarcely show quality row of caulis and practically leaped across the next patch arriving at the outside privvy in almost a bound. I was about to whisper 'My God, the dogs are in there' (the trailer not the lavatory) when a woman of maybe fifty with curlers in her hair, teeth noticeable only by their absence, and a sort of white greasy mess covering her face appeared in the doorway of the house with her mouth ajar. Bob leaped back startled by the apparition. 'Me Dad's in the lavatory,' she screamed, as near to hysteria as damn it is to swearing. I tried tapping on the door and uttering in a cajoling voice 'It's all right, Mister' (the name threw me a little)—'it's only an accident, there's no need to panic,' but only a low moan seemed to be coming from the dark sanctuary of the privvy. I tried the coaxing tone a few more times and then in panic resorted to lying on the floor under the gap of the lavatory door shouting, 'It's all right, Mister' (again thrown by the name). 'You should be ashamed of yourself' shouted a similarly curlered, white-faced virago two doors up and a few powerful looking husbands appeared to reinforce their wives' comments. Bob kicked me slightly, 'Let's pull the bloody thing out of here and hop it.' 'Me Dad's too terrified to come out,' screamed the white-faced one and nasty sneers of 'pervert' and 'weirdo' seemed forthcoming as I shouted soothing words at the pair of boots that were the only things visible under the loo door. Slowly and with great effort we towed the trailer away from the loo through garden one and through the cauliflower patch of garden two, the owner of which was still standing there, mouth open, hoe in hand, stunned by the whole event. 'We'll pay for the damage,' we bleated as we tugged the trailer out on to the road to the chants of 'You should be ashamed of yourself!' from the massed bands of cold-creamed faced harridans that now appeared like mushrooms from everywhere. Shamefacedly we coupled up and drove off hurriedly towards our night's venue, wondering just how many dogs we had left after the collisions with fences one and two, and the brick-built geriatric's toilet, but we didn't stop to check until we reached David's place. With trembling hands we prised open the catch holding the door, expecting to find cadavers of dogs falling out like bodies from wardrobes in an Agatha Christie play, but by some miracle not one dog was damaged by the crash. Omega menaced Pagan with increased fury, as if Pagan had been responsible for the whole business.

Curiously, Omega never worked better than the night of the collision, which goes to prove my theory 'It's not the playing fields of Eton that won us Waterloo—it's the contact with those outside privvies that instils courage and tenacity of the British public.' That's my theory and I'm sticking to it.

An incredible snatch catch about to be staged.

The Giant Buck of No. 10 Shed

Giants are rare in the animal kingdom, and I mean rare. Oh, I admit hunters tell tales of 13 lb hares caught with monotonous regularity, and 20 lb foxes are commonplace in the mild-and-bitter hunting grounds of many worthies, but if people tell the truth, such specimens are rarely seen and seldom if ever caught. There is an optimum size for each species, an ideal size determined by an aeon of savage testing. Those specimens which were larger than the ideal size were invariably too slow or deficient in some other way to weather the troublesome process of survival while those below the optimum size for a species, the puny, the dwarf, the pygmy-type specimens were simply not up to the competition and therefore not able to perpetuate their kind. Take for instance the average, healthy wild rabbit: 2½–3 lb in weight, a great little athlete, able to outpace, to outduck, to outweave nearly all its predators, able and often more than willing to live on poor herbage in winter and gifted with a curious though unpleasant little habit of being able to reingest its pellets to get the maximum goodness out of its diet. All in all, its size of mouth, its habits, are ideally suited to support its 2½–3 lb bodyweight—which to put it mildly is a pretty deft piece of construction from the workshop of the Almighty. So let's throw a spanner into the works and see what happens. An 8 lb agouti (which means wild coloured in scientific terms) buck rabbit escapes from a hutch and hightails it into the wild, going native so to speak with the wild rabbits of the district. On the surface of it, it appears as though he's an odds-on favourite for survival amongst the rabbits of the nearby warren. In next to no time he is wary of man and has become athletic enough to avoid the attentions of most dogs during the daylight hours. Ladbrokes would certainly not be willing to take any bets on his chances against rival bucks only a third of his weight and such a buck would put up one hell of a show against a stoat or even a large hob ferret, for, curiously, tame rabbits are rarely as afraid of mustelid predators as their wild brothers. Haagerdoorn believes tame rabbits are hare/rabbit hybrids—but there is no proof or reason behind his theory. Yes, indeed, the escapee seemingly has a lot going for him and, on the surface of it it seems likely that he will stamp his type and size on all the wild does in the district and 8 lb bunnies will be the norm rather than the exception. Yes, apparently he has a lot going for him—or has he? If he has to gobble down enough food to support his giant frame he has to forage to exist on the same rough herbage as his smaller brethren and here's the rub, I'm afraid—he has only one mouth to ingest the huge quantity of food required to sustain his large weight. For a month or two, particularly in summer, he will survive long enough to impregnate a large number of does perhaps, and the next season will see large, more powerful rabbits grazing the land around the warren, but such rabbits don't do as well as one might expect and after a generation or two the average size of the conies drifts back to the usual 2½–3 lb. Big is not always best in the animal or plant kingdom where the problem of survival is concerned. A chap called H. G. Wells once wrote a book called *The Food of the Gods*—a wonderful piece of science fiction wizardry about a scientist who designs a food to produce giganticism in all species, chickens the size of an ostrich, cats the size of sabre-toothed tigers, education officers with brains of normal size, etc, and when threatened with society at its bureaucratic and most stupid best, threatens to fire canisters of the food into the sewers and produce rats the size of calves.

Assuming Wells's curious chemical could have produced, the first generation of the hundredweight rats which would have been pretty fearsome and would have created carnage in the streets as well as enormous holes in the skirting board; but such monsters would find it hard to survive on the midden piles and two or three generations would find quite ordinary 12 ounce honest-to-goodness *rattus norvegicus* living where those giants once stalked. Yes, a giant's, like a policeman's, lot is not a happy one, which, after a massive piece of scientific hogwash, brings me to the meat of the tale.

Now it is one hell of an admission for a person who has been paid by the state to study or at least make a half-hearted lunge at trying to be an academic, that the only thing I have to my credit for my forty-odd years on this planet is the fact that I believe I've taken the biggest buck rat ever caught. Admittedly there isn't all that much competition for the 'biggest rat ever taken stakes', and I've never even sniffed a contender on the Roy Castle Show, and it must seem pathetic that a grown man has only this to boast about, but there it is. I believe I've taken the biggest buck rat, and, more to the point, I have photographs to prove it. What the heck, there are a million more freaks in the world

The Giant Buck of No. 10 shed.

who boast that they have the longest neck, or lunatics who make the Record Breakers for having the largest lead weights inserted in their noses, so in the light of this, having taken the largest brown rat ever doesn't seem all that way out a boast.

I wasn't the first to see him, not by a long chalk. Baker, a fellow teacher, one of the few in the profession to do their own thing and say 'nuts' to the world, who had hunted that farm pretty nigh every night for two years, first mentioned him. The morning in question—a time when most teachers are only too keen to get away from the kids—Baker stirred his coffee pensively and said almost apologetically, 'D'you know Bri, I saw the biggest rat I've ever seen last night.' He gestured with his hands to indicate a brute of preposterous size, a veritable Primo Carera of rats. My raised eyebrows caused him to shrug his shoulders and mutter, 'I knew you wouldn't believe me,' and drifted off to teach 3U: a somewhat difficult class full of tattooed louts, vicious street brawlers and foul mouths—and the boys in the class were just as bad. To be honest, I disregarded Baker's statement, for nothing makes a man more prone to exaggeration than a rat. Even reliable, sane and truthful men are prone to extraordinary exaggerations when it comes to rats. Reader, I beg you to try an experiment. Walk into a pub, any pub, ranging from the domino and crib playing establishments of the Black Country to the swish 'we cater for junior executive gin and it' pubs of Solihull and just bring up the topic of rats. The subject will cause a massive surge of interest in the Black Country and you will be the centre of conversation until the towels are put up. In Solihull while things are perhaps a mite different, but after the supercilious smirks have worn off the faces of the teeny-bop executives (one brain among three and a glance at them will convince one why British industry is on its knees), and the Martini-sipping bored wives have shown their expected disdain, once again you are the centre of conversation. OK, so you don't manage to pull a great number of women if you go on about rats (I suppose golf buffs are just as boring), and too much fervour and interest in rodents will usually qualify you for a strait-jacket, but once in a while try the experiment.

'Rats, you've seen nothing like it', snorts a slightly rude Jaguar-owner, 'until you've been to Knowle' (a posh, snooty rat-free area in Solihull), and then with a show of hands he indicates a beast which must have given rise to the Surrey puma legend. 'Shot the biggest bastard you've ever seen near the golf club,' and then once again stretched his span to describe a beast that would have needed an Exocet missile to slow it up. 'One night', mutters the third domino player on the right, desperate to enter the conversation now that he realises that all the two's have been played and he's got a hand full of unsuitable spots, 'One night I saw them on the move,' he explains, giving the obligatory shudder expected of one who has witnessed a mass migration. 'Moving in a column.' All ale glasses are frozen and the drinkers remain petrified, frozen like amateur dramatics players having an unsuccessful bash at *Winterset*. 'All led by a giant King rat this big.' He stretches his hands to describe a giant. The Jaguar-owner smiles—it's the rat he slew with his Exocet. 'Thousands of 'em,' continues the raconteur, leaping to his feet for another half, thereby toppling a pile of his mate's dominoes, an action which automatically merits a re-deal or whatever they do in dominoes.

Well, rats of such colossal dimensions don't exist, and, if they did and still possessed the average Mr Ordinary brown rat's ability to fight, would drive off a Baskerville-destroying Great Dane, let alone a terrier. Furthermore, beasts of this size which had *rattus norvegicus*'s propensity for burrowing would just about play hell below Brum and the natives would wake early one morning to find Erdington to

Northfield slowly sinking like a Sherlock Holmes fugitive ending it all in the Grimpton Mire. Believe me, reader, if such monsters were found in Knowle (my God, Knowle of all places), I'd quick as a flash inseminate an Irish Wolfhound with Vampire's semen, breed a pack of hell-bent colossuses, and then get one of those six months' sick notes that seem to have dogged the teaching profession in 1982. Alas, they do not exist (the rats, not the sick notes), so I still trudge to school like a Shakespearean schoolboy.

Next ludicrous legend about to pop—the hoary old one about the King rat—is a stupid story heard so often that I believe that not only should every house have one, but every home actually does. Rats just don't have monarchs which lead them on each and every migration—and migrations rarely, if ever, take place. True, colonies of ever pregnant does and grey youngsters are dominated by a powerful and often very aggressive buck, a buck which will see off any rival foolish enough to move in, but to call such a male a King is stretching it a bit. Migrations—why, all one has here is a colony ousted from the lairs by floods, excavations or suchlike. Sixteen rats moving down a road at night must seem pretty nightmarish to the ratophobe, and let's face it, most of us are ratophobes, so sixteen grey immature rats on the move scurrying furtively down an ill-lit street quickly become a scene from Nosferatu.

Baker, however, is a different kettle of fish, a keen naturalist, a trained scientist and one of the calmest men I have ever encountered. Thus I began to follow up the story, intrigued by Baker's tale of the rat the size of a small cat. We discussed the matter over the dinner table during my lunch break and very soon by some amazing coincidence we had the table to ourselves! 'Yes,' replied Baker, 'I saw him feeding with a colony of young greys near the bagging shed,' and for the first time I began to doubt Baker's knowledge of rats. He saw my disbelief and muttered 'Please yourself,' and ambled off to the dinner hatch where a batch of third years were scraping their compulsory parsnips into the swill tray thereby confirming my opinion that on-one in the world likes parsnips and they are grown simply to waste. 'With some greys?' I questioned, but Baker had vanished to separate a squabble between two third-year blonde girls—a brave man is Baker, believe me.

Well I had forgotten all about Baker and his huge rat and gone into one of my blacker than black moods, near suicidal depressions which are induced by my failure as a teacher and my own personal sense of inadequacy. Black depressions of this sort make me retreat from the world and take refuge away from other people in such a manner that even my close friends begin to doubt my sanity. When the manic depressive pendulum tends to hit the depressive side of the scale too often I rip out my phone and literally go into hiding from all but my closest friends. The week in question was a bad one, depression-wise. If one is unorthodox in the teaching profession (and by unorthodox I mean not conforming to the rather boring norm but keeping ferrets and dogs), one is considered infra-dig and suffers the universally accepted punishment for being different, by being not only ostracised but harassed. So once again I was phased out of the time table, and prepared to spend a year kicking my heels and trying to find something to do to prevent me becoming completely deranged. School became hell, for I am by nature a hyperactive, and the boredom of having literally nothing to do began to etch into my sanity, wearing away my self-confidence and making the pendulum literally stick on the depressive side of the swing.

I phoned David that night from a public call box—I'd disconnected my own phone about three days previously—and asked if I could hunt his farm nightly or even go over there to watch the rats in the headlights of the car. Rats have so much in common with humans. Both species are brutal, though man seems to have the edge as far as brutality goes. Allow an overpowering father to dominate his boy and, whoops! you have an up and coming homosexual too unsure of himself to even talk to women. Likewise when a really dominant male rat becomes master of a colony, one finds the outskirts of the colony full of celibate males cleaning and grooming each other like hairdressers in a Swedish 'unsuitable for adults' film. A menopausal woman can change from being all sweetness and light to a harridan when the hormones begin to go awry, and a female rat just topping the year and approaching senility will entice young males and deliver the carotid bite which not only tends to quench the youngster's fire but extinguishes his life in a trice. Otherwise rats are fairly pleasant animals, and to call the venomous struggle to make it to director/headmaster/chief of staff or what have you, a rat race, is one hell of an insult to good old *rattus norvegicus*. So when I'm depressed I simply go and watch the rats playing around the fowl pens, manifesting all the qualities one associates with humans—the poor sods!

I leant against the side of the van watching a colony feeding and cavorting, the young making rather insane little 'puts' to get back to the warren for no reason in particular, other than to accustom themselves to the escape routes should problems present themselves, and then, quite suddenly, I saw Baker's rat, a grey, feeding and playing with a band of maybe a dozen other young greys, acting as foolishly as they were, as immature and skittish as his fellows, with nothing to distinguish him from his brethren apart from the fact that he was the size of a four month old kitten. He must have sensed my movements, and with ears pricked he began to clean himself nervously, ready to flee to his warren as soon as danger presented itself. I clapped my hands, eager to see him run and he raced ponderously off to the warren a foot or so behind his nimble and smaller siblings. I had never seen his like before and to say that I shall never see his like again would be jumping the gun, but damn it, rats of this size are extremely rare.

Temporarily all thoughts of the misery of school vanished and I took to wondering what caused such a freak, what distortion of genes produced such a colossus, what incredible divine prank caused such a beast to be born. He was five times the size of his siblings and still grey—a stripling of maybe eight weeks old with still time to grow. Excitedly I pondered on the size of the brute, and speculated on my

David's farm, a view from the air.

future hunting at the farm. Surely such a brute would overcome all the other bucks and become master of the warren, and being master thereby improve the size of the rats on the establishment to the extent that only the gamest of my dogs would dare to hunt the place. Had I witnessed the first of a new and terrible species of rodent, *rattus norvegicus novus* or maybe *rattus giganticus*, but such thoughts were not only absurd but unscientific. Big is not always best. During my military service I was placed in the next bed to a huge chap called Murphy, a seven foot giant from the Midlands, a genial, gentle boy without a streak of malice in his body, a quiet lad who became the billet whipping boy, bullied beyond the bounds of human decency by all and sundry. No, there was nothing to suggest that my giant rat had the get up and go to assert himself and become even a breeding buck, let alone the dominant buck of the colony.

It may seem curious that I had no desire to hunt and catch my giant, but I have never been a trophy hunter. In fact one of the most repulsive sights I have ever seen is the photograph of a tiny bespectacled hunter—the epitome of the nineteen-sixties style film about henpecked husbands, perched incongruously on the carcass of a huge bull elephant—a mountain of animal flesh slain by a pathetic myopic man and his high-technology elephant rifle. Likewise the sight of a gigantic eland head on a trophy hunter's wall sickens me as did the pursuit of a white fox by numerous heavy-booted Walsall riff-raff, when the beast appeared in my district last year. To be different, large or unusually coloured is inviting death so it seems, and I believe that white blackbirds are rare in the world, not so much because they don't blend with their environment so much as because their unusual colour invites some buffoon to shoot them. Heck, I'm different myself and I've taken bad times aplenty because of it. Thus I decided to let my giant live, and monitor his progress. What the hell, a rat watch is no more ludicrous than a badger watch; but a rat is not a badger and no rat, particularly a huge ponderous brute, is likely to invite sympathy.

I watched him many times during the boring mind-destroying timetableless months which followed; and I almost protected him, I suppose, simply because I felt a curious affinity with him. Both of us would be the objects of ridicule and dislike, him for his huge size and me for my odd interests, and in time I knew that he too would be the focal point of persecution simply because he was different. A month after our first encounter, his fur had changed from grey to brown and he became a mature male, capable of breeding, but reluctant to leave the bachelor lairs to do battle with the large scabrous buck which ruled the bank colony. He developed an odd guinea-pig like look as he sat on his hindlegs cleaning himself, and at one time I considered trapping him to keep him as a curiosity, and even maybe to catch him a few does to allow him to start a rat colony on a farm nearer my house. I scrapped the idea of trying to breed a super-rat, however, not because the act of transferring live rats to another district is probably illegal, but simply because any caged rat of any sort is more ill-at-ease in captivity than even a wild caught finch; and I had grown oddly attached to my giant.

A working terrier show loomed on the horizon and much as I dislike such gatherings, their noise, their bitterness and the sickening macho lads who parade with a dozen or so terriers on leads defying the world to even look at them—or maybe simply inviting comment by their curious appearance, I decided to go if only to break the horrid boredom and inactivity of three months of literally sitting on my backside in the staffroom, hoping and praying that some member of the staff would be away and I could spend my time taking their lessons. I had, at last, experienced the all-time low, not only in my teaching career but also in my own morale, and that Friday, while making another pointless trip to school, I chanced upon a road accident rabbit cadaver on Pipe Hill and envied it its fate.

So Saturday came, and to break the awful monotony of the week, I attended the terrier and lurcher show; but if I hoped it would ease my depression, then I was mistaken. I never show dogs, as I feel rather embarrassed by the prospect of holding a dog to be examined by the judge, and even more embarrassed by prancing around the show ring with a dog tugging at its leash. However, the people one meets at these shows are often interesting in a bizarre sort of way, and the incredible lies some of them tell have to be taken with a large block of salt. Hare-killing lurchers which can kill every hare that gets up abound. Terriers, usually large, oversized blacks, known quite wrongly as Patterdales, which have slain a thousand or so foxes (and curiously are now for sale for forty or so pounds) are paraded around by unsavoury characters whose arms are usually covered in tattoos and whose ears are ringed with enough gold to suggest that at night their Mums and Dads made them sleep with their heads in the safe. More irritating still are 'the challengers', boys scarcely old enough to shave, yet knowing all they need to know about terriers, lurchers and indeed everything. I hate these idiots with their flamboyant boasts, their irritating abrasive manner and their desire to become instantly famous or notorious by bringing down some experienced terrier keeper or other. Frank Buck, an expert terrier man, has the knack of shaking off these idiots, but I lack Frank's panache and sometimes end up competing against these fools in rat-killing contests usually with the odds stacked against me with as many as six dogs matched against my best terrier. To cut a long story short, I finished up the day being barracked and baited by three worthies with over-sized fell terrier dogs, suitable for bear-baiting perhaps, but at the cut-and-thrust sport of rat hunting far too large and ponderous to be a threat to Omega. I avoided the baiting fairly well and prepared to leave the show quietly, unobtrusively, and in as discreet and as cowardly a manner as possible, but they sensed my move and were waiting at the gates, baiting and barracking louder than ever. I suppose that as a writer I must set myself up as an Aunt Sally just waiting to be put down; but after about twenty minutes of taking all the flack they could throw, my depression was finally replaced by a cold fury and I agreed to play Omega against three Lakelands for £100 a terrier, their combined scores being totalled against hers. Frankly, in spite of the odds, it wasn't really that much of a contest. Omega weighed 12 lb, her best weight, she was whippet thin and her coat shone like glass. Their dogs were a motley bunch and all bore the scars of some badly organised badger hunts where a dog behind the victim pushed the poor devil into the jaws of the badger. One terrier, a large red, was overweight, with bad eczema, and another had lost one side of its jaws, while the third, a sixteen-inch giant, had seen little work and was nearly thirty pounds in weight. We shook hands, agreed to the wager and parted company and frankly I never expected to see them again, for once a macho boy has shown a crowd he's not afraid of anyone, in the very best infant school story book style, he is never seen again—a state which frankly suits me fine. But I had the oddest feeling this band of machos would turn up at the venue in three weeks' time.

 Well, I had forgotten about this business and went on with the usual humdrum existence which has characterised my life, the bed, work routine, and Monday, Thursday and Saturday nights at the poultry farm. Curiously, my depression had lifted somewhat, though things in school were worsening by the day. I have never been able to resign myself to defeat, and now a sort of fire had begun inside me and I became prepared to fight the system rather than simply duck the punches. Each night found me at David's and most nights I saw the

Frank Buck.

A live catch.

giant which lived in the bank at the rear of Number 10 shed.

A rat's life is short by any standards and they flash from infancy through a furious puberty to scabrous senility in a matter of twelve months, like a David Bellamy film showing a flower blossoming, fruiting, seeding and dying almost before the viewer's eyes. My rat had grown no bigger since moulting his grey coat and had begun to develop a dusty moth-eaten look, like an Oxfam musquash coat. In this state, he would have lived out his rather meaningless celibate life, probably becoming mangy, scabrous and decrepit before the following spring, had not destiny become unkind to him.

On the Monday a load of ducklings were delivered to the farm, quaint yellow, fluffy creatures which would grow into seven pound paranoid creatures in eight weeks or so. Now ducklings are easy to rear if the pen is rat proof, but the trouble is it is difficult to make the pen rat proof if a rat decides otherwise. In New York the rats gnawed through the ferro-concrete walls of a sewer; so the mere wood and netting of a poultry pen didn't prove any problem, and by Tuesday morning over a hundred tiny pitiful cadavers littered the pen. Now a rat attack on ducklings is enough to sicken anyone and make the most ardent rat enthusiast reach for the Warfarin. Baby ducklings are literally torn to pieces while they are still alive, the rat setting to work on the throat and tearing into the thin, almost cartoon shaped necks, and waiting for the duckling to topple. More often than not they simply slay their victims and hurry on to the next without so much as eating a morsel of their prey. A really voracious rat on the rampage will see off a hundred or so ducklings at a sitting and even a casual sort of rat will create mayhem on a batch of week or so old birds. Few rats attack ducklings above four weeks old, possibly because they are a little large for a rat to consider as prey, and partly because they are fast enough to evade the attentions of a rat.

What causes this near-maniacal attack? Rats will race through batches of day-old chicks to have a whack at ducklings. Well, there are many theories, most of which are a bit crackpot, to say the least. Perhaps the smell of ducklings is irresistible to rats, and rats do rely quite a lot on their sense of smell. Perhaps the insane fluttering triggers off some reaction in the rat; but day old chicks are just as dithery and witless, yet they usually escape the attentions of a rampaging rodent. One thing is certain; few bucks indulge this orgy of slaughter and blood. The culprits are invariably does, does with young, pregnant does and does about to draw bedding; but without further ado and without even asking I knew which rat would be held responsible for the slaughter in the duck pens. By dint of examining the gap in the wire through which the rat had entered the duck pen, a gap which was a mere slit, I deduced my giant could never have climbed through such a hole. The star-like bloodstained footprints on the concrete floor were average-sized whereas my giant wore size thirteen boots; but I knew he'd be held responsible.

Quite suddenly, biblical tales and fairy stories took on a different meaning for me. Jack the Giant Killer ceased to be the super-hero and became a sly little trophy hunter out to bag an ungainly and rather stupid giant, much like my bespectacled elephant hunter, one foot astride the carcass of a fallen bull elephant. David became the slayer of some harmless circus freak who, reluctant as he was, had been pushed into battle simply because of his size. Chances are Goliath and Fee Fi Fo Fum were simply antique harmless versions of my friend Murphy, just out there waiting to be bagged by trophy hunters who would slip into folklore as supermen. My buck had fed on meal from Number 10 shed, ignoring the hens, and the duck barn was a star's flight from his territory, yet he was held responsible for the slaughter. Hence, to keep the peace and the ratting nights on the farm, I reluctantly set out to kill him.

Saying is one thing, but doing is another. A dozen times I could have killed him during his grey infancy; once I was so close to him that I could have brought an end to his life with a deft kick. Battle, ratting alone and refusing to be boxed up in the trailer, upended the poor devil only a week before; yet, squealing and kicking, he had somehow evaded her *coup-de-grace* and scampered down the rabbit-sized rat warren to safety. Now we were hell-bent on taking the poor devil, however, even the sight of him became uncommon. At one time, scarcely a day went by when I didn't chance upon a few pence in the gutter in Lichfield, but when I was on my uppers financially and searching the town for dropped coins—a little act called stealing by finding, Mo calls it—I found nothing. And now, when I was deliberately out to catch the old devil, he seldom appeared and, when he did, he was on the very limits of my beam a yard or so away from his lair. We hunted every night merely to get the reputed duckling-slayer, and though our total of kills was enormous somehow the old devil evaded us. So preocuppied was I with taking him that I quite forgot the challenge from the two machos and was unaware that the 'meet' was the day after Keith Ruston was coming to photograph a rat hunt.

It was an evening like any other, I suppose. The meet assembled at my house at 9 o'clock, the copious doses of black, badly made tea, the chit chat about the events of the week and previous hunts, the crating of the dogs, and by 10 p.m. we were on our way to the farm, Beltane rumbling a warning at Omega and Ruston doing all sorts of technical stuff to stop his camera lenses steaming up. He'd worked with us before and enjoyed the hunt, so he knew roughly what to do and was so popular with the boys that even Hank and Ginger didn't try to flick a live rat at him. Well, we disgorged from my foetid van, uncrated the dogs, dealt Omega and Beltane a quick slap each to prevent a cut and thrust battle, and in next to no time we were settling the team in the plucking house, hunting a few witless rats out of the crates.

We took a fair haul of rats that evening, and by the time we reached Number 10 Shed, Ginger was tottering around carrying 60 lb of rats for ferret food. 'They'll never eat this many,' he moaned, 'let's go home.' By now it was raining heavily and I sympathised with the poor kid, whose sodden sack of rats was growing heavier by the minute. Still, a hunt is a hunt, and rather than be termed a fine weather

Omega stations herself.

sportsman, I flung open the doors of No. 10 Shed, grouped the dogs, and switched on the light. Lights, action, and all that's missing is the music! Omega immediately stationed herself. Beltane, infirm yet still utterly reliable, marked. Vampire flashed under the battery cages, and Blaze and Battle began hunting enthusiastically but not well. Ruston's flash lit up the shed like daylight from time to time as the squeaks and squeals drowned Ginger's moans about the ever-increasing weight of the sack. We must have spent ten or twenty minutes in the shed with Ruston photographing every move of Omega, and Ginger complaining bitterly, while Hank prodded the piles of dung below the battery cages to dislodge the rats. Quite suddenly I saw Hank leap backwards and stand stock still in the alleyway separating the two stands of battery cages. He stood, mouth ajar, simply pointing at the top tray and there was no reason for me to ask him why. I knew what he'd seen. Crouched in the chicken dung, cleaning himself in a state of anxiety sat my giant, as big as a half-grown cat, rubbing his ears with his paws, while his smaller brethren crouched beside him also cleaning themselves. Cleaning has a soothing action on rats, much as nail-biting eases the tension in a human being. He sat there illuminated by my beam, a large, slightly scabrous rat, near senility, a rat who more than likely had lived out his celibate life without so much as harming a living thing.

I took the stick from Hank's hand, and still keeping the brute in the beam, began to move him along the trays towards the spot where Omega stood stock still and waiting for the cascade of rats about to plummet to the ground to get to the escape holes. Twice my giant scrambled over the stick as if he knew what fate awaited him on the floor, while all the while Vampire worked the chicken dung under the bottom tray. Rats are by nature rather shy and nervous creatures, and a grinding war of nerves of prodding them with sticks and shining a beam in their eyes eventually causes most of them to panic and make the fatal mistake of trying to make a bolt for it. Eventually my giant too panicked and came off the trays almost into the jaws of Omega.

She stood there watching his huge bulk scramble down the netting wire, cages, her mouth open and her eyes wide as if in disbelief at the bulk of the clumsy brute trying to scrabble to the floor. He touched the floor and flashed for his bolt hole, a hole grown smooth and greasy by the passage of generations of rodents. There was no way Omega could miss him, she had but to bend her head to strike him, she had but to side step to prevent him reaching sanctuary, but she stood stock still, not moving a muscle, her eyes averted as if she was trying not to see the monster trying to escape. It all happened in a trice. Vampire flashed from under the trays and cut off the retreat of the giant, snatching at it as he did so. For the first time in his life the giant retaliated and buried his teeth into the bone of Vampire's lower jaw, locking like a bulldog while Vampire rolled and battered the monster to get in a finishing bite. How long the battle lasted is difficult to estimate. Sufficient to say Ruston's camera flashed six or seven times during the fight. A 2 lb 4 ounce rat is no match for a stocky twelve pound grappler of a terrier and the outcome of the fight was clear from the start. Vampire eventually brought his teeth together across the old devil's back and began to shake, still batting the rat against the side of the shed, shaking and crunching it long after it was dead while all the while Omega stood back and watched the spectacle. It was the first time she'd ever let me down. I felt sick with worry at the following night's contest. Ginger prised the giant from Vampire's blood be-speckled jaws and we sent the cadaver away to be weighed, knowing, or at least guessing, we'd killed a world record rat, but I felt little pride

A bad scrimmage in No. 10 shed.

A senile buck meets its end.

in my catch, merely a terrible apprehension that tomorrow night Omega might once again jib and refuse to take a rat, leaving me wondering whether the next night would see me begging around my friends to pay the £300 in betting money.

I need not have worried. Next night she trounced the opposition 57 to 8, and I put a down payment on my tiny Fiat that Saturday, vowing that never again would I be cajoled or bullied into such a contest, but, as I am always being told, I am extremely weak-willed and like Oscar I resist anything except temptation.

A Night at the Opera?

I like Roy, at least I think I like Roy. He is articulate, academic and one of my closest friends. He is bright, normally full of common sense, honest to the point of being a prude, and totally reliable. He is also a fiend, with a sense of humour one could only class as ghoulish; and, while I could trust him with my house and what little money I possess, I certainly would not trust him with my life, particularly if the manner of my demise could be classed as anything he would consider humorous—such as falling into a blast furnace, being attacked by something large and carnivorous, being cut up by a circular saw or even garrotted. Come to think of it I'd be hard pressed to find a way of 'ending it all' which Roy did not consider to be humorous, for as I've said, Roy has no gentle side to his nature, for Roy is a fiend. So having introduced you to the principal character of this rather unpleasant chapter—as they say in the very best women's magazines—*Now read on.*

At that time I was earning a dishonest bob or two supposedly teaching in a rather curious little sec mod supplementing my £115 a month by advertising for Hebrew Arabic or what have you for translation, and attracting a whole host of oddballs who mistook my ads for 'French lessons' or some Asiatic equivalent. The phone would ring, a whispered voice would talk about ear muffs and savage correction, and a few other unpleasant little things one reads about but the mind refuses to believe. Just now and again I'd get wizards— not boys' comics, real wizards with whole books of grimoires (books of spells) to translate and one even produced a Hebrew type spell and recipe which guaranteed him eternal life and after making me promise not to remember the spell and potion and follow him into foreverness (not an attractive thought, believe me), he departed, probably planning where he would take his holidays in the year 3000. Another such character read my ad and appeared at my house with his 'book'. He was a shabby macintoshed figure with a grimy skin and the deathly pallor of one who is either desperately ill or enjoying an active if vicarious life. The 'book' turned out to be written in Swedish—a language about which I know nothing, in spite of watching the Muppets regularly, but it turned out that the book didn't really need translation, concerned as it was with a very athletic scantily clad young lady called Helga and a very large extremely tractable Dobermann Pinscher called Jarl. (Strange, I'd always regarded Dobermanns as unfriendly creatures.) The book however, written in large Janet and John type print for the discerning semi-literate pervert, was in Swedish; so after examining the book for a mere seven hours I decided it was beyond me. (You don't learn such things in the canine obedience classes, mate, I can tell you.) I let him go. But again I've missed the point of the tale which concerns Roy (a fiend), and a night at the opera—I think I'd better explain before the book goes back on the library shelf and another dissatisfied reader joins the ranks.

Well, at this time, I was really trying to scratch up some cash to take out and impress an opera singer called Maria Endez ('Real name's probably Martha Scroggs,' sniffed Mo disdainfully), a good-looking Spanish type lady who sang with a Mediterranean accent and spoke reasonably broad Harpenden—not that I've anything against Harpenden mind you, except perhaps that in 1788 a chap from Harpenden actually ate a live cat for a bet, but that was a long time ago and most people have probably forgotten about it. Accent aside, Maria was quite something to look at, and while I couldn't help thinking about that cat whenever she spoke, she had a fantastic singing voice and Carmen-type looks to match. Mo met her once, and glancing at my scruffy appearance sneered, 'S'pose they like a bit of rough now and again, helps them with the high notes maybe.' I've never really understood what he meant by this. Maria however was anything but a snob and one night while I was eating the remains of her Chinese take-away (I wasn't up to buying two at this time), she said apropos of nothing in particular, 'You know (that bloody cat flashed into view again), Phillip, my leading man would love to come on a rat hunt.'

Now this may seem a little strange to anyone who has not been on one of my organised rat hunts—and there must be at least fifty-two million people in Britain who haven't, but we've had an amazing collection of people who've asked to come. The most common type of applicant is, I admit, the macho circus type artiste whose heavy boots are complemented by his rather nice earrings and somewhat bizarre tattoos. (One had 'Hello' tattooed on his lower lips so that he had only to brush his mouth with his hand to express his pleasure at seeing you.) There are maniacs who usually volunteer themselves to 'Come up and sort out my rats.' Other applicants have been near-lunatics who've eaten live mice washed down with Guinness (which didn't do the mice much good) to a ghoul who offered me an amputated human hand for my ferrets.

On the credit side we had the lead singer from a group called Scaramouche, a fantastic looking woman with green hair and a cockscomb of red (OK if you like that sort of thing I suppose—and most of us did), a few TV celebs, Frank Sheardown and a flyweight champion from Mexico, a diminutive mite who looked as though a good rat would get the better of him yet who cut a swathe through most American flyweights and bantamweights. Now it may surprise the reader to know that we turn down ninety-nine out of every hundred applicants, and even those who come don't always last the course. Yet people are seemingly fascinated with the blood and death that goes hand in hand with a good class rat hunt. The macabre fascinates the average Mr and Mrs, I suppose. Just go to a circus and watch a nervous woman eagerly, excitedly and obscenely sucking her ice lolly while a trapeze artist flies overhead performing weird and wonderful things while the whole crowd are hoping and praying that the climax of the act will be a very unpleasant mash of spangled pulp and sawdust. Likewise, quaint old ladies of the type who invite one back for tea and muffins will sit glued to the box watching some famous surgeon hacking his way into no-one in particular to extract a piece of nastiness which would turn a Durham navvy green. Just watch the TV viewing figures! James Bond would be hard pressed to keep a solitary viewer if his film was on at the same time as a particularly nasty little epic called 'Birth of a Baby'—a film which would find me hastily diving for the off button before I raced screaming to the 'loo'.

As I've said, man is a macabre devil, but for Phillip, Don José to Maria's Carmen, a rat hunt was to be a bit much for him—and that's putting it mildly. Thursday night, and we all assembled at the cottage. 'What's he like?' sniffed Porky. (Porky always sniffed—'Don't 'ave him in your writing room,' said Mo, 'half your manuscript will disappear up his hooter'.) 'What's he like?' sniffed Porky again, irritated by the fact that everyone always ignored him. 'I don't know, Porky,' I replied politely; 'all I know is Maria asked him to come.' Roy and I continued to peruse the evening paper for TV viewing ignoring Porky. 'I know a man', Porky went on, totally out of context and trying to attract attention 'who,'—he thought a moment to get the maximum impact from the statement—'who in a pub, bit off a peacock's head.' My ears pricked slightly, and I was dying to ask what in hell a peacock was doing in a pub, but it was standard practice to ignore Porky, so we continued to peruse the papers for something to occupy our minds (and shut off Porky for a while) while we readied ourselves for the rat hunt. 'This man', Porky continued, unruffled by our lack of response, 'had a snake tattooed round and round his leg, and its head disappeared . . .' 'Don't want to hear, Porky,' said Roy, switching on the telly (a pity, as I did want to hear, but we were ignoring Porky that night so I didn't press the matter).

Viewing-wise it was poor that night. The Beeb had a film about the French resistance and the Gestapo—the sort of thing I hate, as I feel so damned inadequate about watching callow youths absorb terrific punishment rather than betray their friends, knowing as I do that the Gestapo would only have to threaten me with a trip to an osteopath or worse still a dentist, to find me making a written statement in triplicate denouncing my mother for being a resistance fighter, a vampire or anything. The other side looked more promising as it was one of those Japanese epics about an atomic test which resurrected some long frozen dinosaur from an iceberg and all hell was let loose. Fire couldn't harm it, bullets bounced off its hide, cannons, anti-tank weapons and bazookas just failed to slow it up—and just when the audience was beginning to wonder why in hell the sods became extinct, the now radioactive monster began systematically devouring the cities of Japan, swimming the Pacific and working his way none too selectively from Seattle to Chicago. Fortunately, just as it had swum the Atlantic Ocean and was about the destroy Barnsley it became allergic to Wrigleys Spearmints and died—a disappointing end perhaps, but anyway I'd seen it before. 'I know a barmaid called Rita,' Porky spat out (all Porky's barmaids are called Rita), 'who put a lizard . . .' 'Shut up, Porky!' we all shouted, deliberately ignoring him, and we were off on the rat hunt.

We pulled up at the farm and the headlights of my very mucky van picked up a swish brand new Porsche—a gleaming red job, every teeny-bop's dream and one that would probably herd in more women than the entire canine cast of *One Man and His Dog*. Out of the Porsche stepped a tall, slightly-built Don José clad in white cords and a very white 30 quid touch Guernsey sweater. 'I fink they call them spats,' said Porky about nothing in particular. We ignored him but I could not help noticing a fierce glint in Roy's eyes, a glint which bespoke that the evening would be a shade different from our run-of-the-mill rat hunts. The apparition in white minced towards us stepping gingerly over a blob of something which had fallen from the trailer and which was liable to stain his brand new shining white shoes. ''E aint right,' said Porky sagely, and I could see what our sage meant. Phillip was not right for the task in hand, and glancing at the evil grin on Roy's face, I had just the merest hint that the evening ahead would be one I would always remember. 'I knew a queer once,' whispered Porky, but we ignored him and introduced ourselves to the immaculate Phillip.

I extended my hand, 'Brian,' I said, 'and this is Roy, who works the trays'—a look akin to blank misunderstanding flitted across Phillip's face—'I used to work as a waiter while on hols from music school' he simpered rather patronisingly, not understanding what the heck working the trays meant, but the scowl on Roy's face boded evil for Phillip from that moment on. I introduced Frank, who slunk into the background. 'And this is Porky, our bagman' (a man who picks up all the dead rats for ferret food). Porky did not shake hands partly because he suspected Phillip of being a sexual deviate but mostly because he was deeply engrossed in picking his nose—an action which caused a look of amazed disbelief from Phillip as he watched Porky's index finger disappear almost from view up his nostrils. 'I wouldn't want 'im touching my rats with those bleeding hands,' sneered Roy. 'No way,' he reiterated, shaking his head to dispel the vision of Porky actively engaged with his nostrils. I glanced across at the clown who by now had a look of near ecstasy spreading across his fat face—I could see what Roy meant about touching 'his rats' and I resolved at the earliest opportunity to get another bagman before an epidemic unknown to the virologist saw off my entire crop of ferrets. 'Young ferrets die off quickly enough without Porky handling their rats,' Roy warned.

Phillip broke the awful tension tactfully. 'Actually,' he said, 'I feel a bit of a fraud coming, as I've a pretty strong fear of rats—it's a sort of basic fear, isn't it?' he fluttered. I groaned aloud closing my eyes in despair. A sort of basic fear! Inside the bar of the Hilton is the place to be if one has a sort of basic fear of rats. October 18th—a time when the corn was down and the rats moving in a manner to deter an enthusiastic Pied Piper, the time of the year when really eager hunters will come from America and Japan just to have a whack at the multitude of rats on the farm—October 18th was not the time for anyone with a sort of basic fear of rats. Basic fear was not a strong enough description for Phillip's fear of rats—far from it.

We glanced around at Porky who was pouring the entire contents of a bag of aniseed balls into his mouth until his cheeks bulged like an over-zealous hamster. Phillip, too, had decided to ignore him. 'Your dogs?' Phillip almost chortled, pointing at the trailer where Vampire's slashed and evil face was just peering through the air space at the top of the door. 'No,' said Roy, who is never one to suffer fools gladly. 'They sort of leaped into the trailer while we stopped at the pub.' But rather than chance further inane comments, I released the pack and set off towards the poultry houses, noticing that Porky had managed to swallow the entire packet of aniseed balls without munching even one. 'His oesophagus is a miracle of engineering,' sneered Roy. 'I aint got a soft gut,' replied Porky sullenly, not understanding a word of Roy's conversation. I made a mental note to drop my laundry in to Madge's and maybe find a normal friend, and set off for Shed No. 1.

'Do you, do you think I could be introduced to the sport gradually?' whispered Phillip, the first seeds of doubt beginning to germinate and sprout like Chinese beans in his mind. I was about to shake my head and say that there was no way he could be introduced to the sport gradually when Roy put in, 'Yeh mate, just stick with me, I see you don't get hurt.' 'Well it wasn't so much hurt,' Phillip bleated rather pitifully, 'but—sort of frightened, I suppose. You see I'm not really used to this sort of thing.' 'Queer,' sneered Porky quietly, pushing an ice slice into his mouth whole without giving it a single bite until he resembled Larry Adler on his way to the infirmary for a harmonicaoptomy. 'You just stick with me,' said Roy slyly, treating Porky to a quick nudge. Omega and Pagan had forgotten their little differences, and Vampire and the rest of the team stood quivering with excitement at the shed doors waiting for all hell to break loose—and, brother, believe me, we had not long to wait; and hell it turned out to be.

Sheds open, lights, action. 'Where shall I stand?' squealed Phillip as Pagan slew a rat near his feet. Battle, disputing the ownership of the cadaver, began to pull at the carcase, grunting and snarling as she did so. Another raced past Phillip and I saw his face crease with disgust as he began to wonder what the hell he was doing here. But most of the dogs were creating mayhem at the bottom of the sheds as Frank was tapping the trays and driving the rats away from the front door towards the end of the building where the main body of the dogs were

Working the trays.

waiting like wolves. Five minutes elapsed while I frantically blocked and stamped on sundry stray rats trying to hightail it back to the door. 'Just look at the prat,' whispered Roy, and glancing round I was treated to the picture of Phillip frozen to the spot, his eyes closed, his body rigid with horror. I shook my head in dismay. The carnage stopped as suddenly as it began. 'OK Porky, pick 'em up,' I shouted, and Porky began to toss the cadavers into the sack. By now Porky had accepted Phillip's dress and little problems and was beginning to chat to the poor devil in quite a friendly manner. 'The one near yer feet,' said Porky trying to be friends, 'ain't got no head,' and he upended the beheaded cadaver to show Phillip who reeled slightly against the wall trying not to look at the spectacle. 'Sometimes,' Porky went on, 'when free or four dogs catch 'old of a dead one, they'll kill 'im and pull 'is legs off. All that's left of this one,' he continued, hurling the carcasses into the sack, 'is the tail, and I ain't taking no tail cos the ferrets won't look at them.' But I had the oddest feeling that Phillip wasn't really interested in the dietary needs and appetites of ferrets as we left the building for Shed No. 2, Porky wielding a bulging sack on which Roy had painted SWAG earlier in the day.

We stopped outside Shed No. 2 and collected the pack around us. A shrill hiss inside the sheds told me that something was amiss: a burst water pipe (chickens in battery houses are on an automatic watering system). I muttered, 'Damn it, the shed will be ankle deep in slurry.' 'Where shall I stand?' whispered Phillip limply. 'In the corner,' whispered Roy. 'Yer said I could do the corners,' said Porky petulantly. 'You're allus promising me the corner an I never pissing get it, do I ever, no never.' I'll explain Porky's enthusiasm for the corner. The corner of number two shed was damaged and broken and the rats automatically raced for this spot in number; and at this time of the year I mean in number. We deliberately prevented the near demented Porky from standing in the corner because, at the first movement of the rats, Porky went berserk, ran amok so to speak, clouting and kicking at rats and dogs, and his wild exuberance had so disturbed one of the puppies that Roy and I had decided never to let Porky work the corners again. Roy silenced Porky with a wave of the hand, as one would calm an erring collie. 'Yer bastard!' whispered Porky sullenly at the allocation of the corner to Phillip. 'I ain't carrying the pissing sack no more then,' and he flung down the swag bag on the concrete allowing various dismembered rats to roll out. Roy gave him a stern look and pointed to the sack and Porky, mumbling various spiteful comments refilled the bag with the rats. 'In the corner,' Roy hissed to Phillip, 'and stay there,' but I knew Phillip was going to be damn nigh as useless as Porky in the corner. So doors open and into the shed with Porky mumbling bitterly about being denied the best places. 'Porky'll 'ave to go' said Frank, the only sane one in the group, as I hit the lights and Roy pushed Phillip into the corner.

Phillip was not ready for the corner, not by a long chalk, and perhaps it would have been wiser to allow the near demented Porky a night of stamping, kicking and screaming, but hindsight is always a whole lot easier isn't it? Lights and stumbling through the slurry, slime into which Phillip's immaculate shoes sank to the ankle, Phillip made the corner and Frank and Roy began to work the trays with a vengance while the dogs went berserk with the teeming rats, feeding just out of range of the wet floor. ''E don't like it, look at 'im,' sneered Porky triumphantly, pushing a sticky jam doughnut into his mouth with blood-stained fingers. (Porky's family had been the only survivors when the plague had hit Burntwood in 1383, so Roy assures me.) ''E don't like it, 'e's useless at corners,' and glancing across I noticed a curious green pallor on Phillip's face and a blob of white spittle appearing on his shuddering bottom lip. 'Told yer I was best

A difficult catch in slurry.

Pagan nails her rat.

for corners,' Porky gloated, handing Phillip his last doughnut—a gesture which for some curious reason Phillip declined to notice. ''E ain't no good at corners,' chortled Porky, 'Roy don't know corners, don't know corners at all.'

The carnage began as Frank and Roy beat towards us and a flock of large rats (if flock is the correct word which I very much doubt) hit the floor and made straight for Phillip, Porky chuntering on about Roy's poor choice for the position. Most were stopped by the dogs, but the second flush reached Phillip, diving past him, scaling his clothes, one even reaching his chest before Omega back-somersaulted and came down with it in his mouth. ''E's letting 'undreds past 'im, look at 'im, look at 'im,' sneered Porky, but his jibe went unnoticed, I fear, for Phillip had not only turned a more attractive shade of green but was beginning to buckle at the knees, and slither down into the unspeakable sludge of fowl dung and meal that was now liberally laced with blood and pieces of rat. One rat dived up Phillip's leg, Beltane killing it at crotch level, and that just about did it. Phillip slithered down into the slurry and lay there face down in the putrid goo. 'Look, he's ruined his spats,' chortled Porky. (I really must check on what Porky meant by spats.) 'Said 'e weren't no good for corners,' but by now the rats were racing over the prostrate Phillip and Pagan had settled on his tightly trousered rump, slaying every rat that tried to make it across Phillip's backside. Vampire crashed into Phillip's face shaking a large scabrous male rat, while another rat attempted to hide under his white Guernsey sweater only to be winkled out by Beltane. I shouted a halt but nobody heeded me as the din and battle raged around us drowning my cries. 'For God's sake help him, Roy, he'll die.' 'A man drownded once in an inch of water,' put in Porky, an avid watcher of Roy Castle's record breakers and Dr Snuggles. Phillip began to groan and attempted to rise as the third wave hit him and Vampire, Beltane, Omega and Pagan set to work on, under and along his body. Phillip groaned and slunk back into the slurry once more. 'Look, 'e's useless in corners,' shouted Porky, 'he ain't even tryin',' his mouth full of another ice slice. We dragged Phillip clear, reviving him with slaps and good wishes while Porky fished around in the slurry for sunken cadavers. 'Ain't wasting these,' he shouted, 'ferrets don't mind shit. Leastways, mine don't,' he put in as a rider.

'You'll be all right next shed,' Roy insisted, reviving our stricken singer. 'Give it a try,' but secretly he realised that Phillip's heart wasn't in it so we left him seated on the dung pile head in hands while we did the rest of the sheds, allowing Porky to fulfil his life-long ambition concerning the corners. We finished, and Porky, groaning under the weight of the swag accompanied us back to the singer. 'If you come next week, it will grow on you,' Roy shouted, but, as Frank said, as the Porsche jerked its way up the yard, 'Yer can see he aint really a ratter,' and he gave Porky a quick slap for bumbling on about the corners.

Of course Phillip didn't come back, though he did send us a very nice letter thanking Roy for his help during the hunt and subsequent unpleasantness. He'd have come again, he explained, but he had a pressing engagement in Hamburg, Paris, Milan or anywhere!! He didn't mention the business to Maria and she never asked about it. Anyway, I finished seeing her the following week. It wasn't that I didn't find her attractive—I did, but every time she spoke, I couldn't stop seeing that chap from Harpenden eating a live cat!

Pagan, the Problems of Water and a Bit More Besides

If asked when Pagan was born, I would be unable to answer without checking in my diary. I tend to lose track of time out here anyway, and events rather than calendar dates seem to record the years as they race by, and when past forty the years pass so quickly. Vampire was born during the year when I damn nigh hanged myself leaping a hedge at night after a roebuck and hit a piece of binder twine—thrown casually in the hedge perhaps, but it just about did for me and left my vocal chords damaged for four months. 'Pleasant like, the silence I mean,' commented Mo. Phoibos, the poisonous little son of Vampire and Beltane, was spawned the year Joan, David's wife, dropped a sliding door on Battle, nearly stunning her and causing her to run off into the night and, like Rumplestiltskin, never to be seen again. Likewise Pagan was born the year the well dried up—or to be more precise Pagan was born because the well dried up, and I'd better explain why, fairly quickly, before the reader loses interest.

When I came here fifteen years ago I wasn't on mains water. In fact I wasn't on any form of water supply and collected my water by diverting the rain from the shed gutters into a huge 1,000 gallon tank. It wasn't a satisfactory system; at least, not when one considers that the rats used the gutter as a step-ladder, urinating and doing something equally unpleasant on the roof. Still, I've always been a bit primitive and lacking in any notions of hygiene and in any case I always boil water before drinking it. Also, I suppose, I must be fairly immune to all the infections 'the air sucks up'; but the time came when the water supply began to get a bit turgid and the contents of the tank resembled the liquid manure barrel of a champion marrow grower, rather than a reservoir of water for human consumption. I couldn't get in to clean the mess out, mess which included for some reason or other a bat, in such a state of decomposition as to prevent identification even by an experienced batologist or whatever someone with a fixation with bats is called. Hence we decided to dig a well, but I fear I use the word 'we' inaccurately.

Digging a well centred in the broken galvanised sheeting hut that I chose to call my ferret pen wasn't an easy matter. Twenty feet down may well attract the seasoned badger digger short of a furious and very energetic whack at brock, but tell the selfsame chap that he has to dig through a similar thickness of clinker, clay and rock to dig a well and you soon get to know who your friends are. Blokes who were regular attenders at the Sunday fox hunts, the Friday and Thursday rat hunts, chaps who made it a point to thrust themselves on me each and every Sunday, winter and summer alike, became scarce. I've always enjoyed my own company and at last I had found a way to ensure I had it. I learned a lot from that experience, believe me. Now when I get a persistent nuisance, one who materialises at the very moment I wish to spend my day alone, all I do is to keep a shovel and a few picks in the porch and the moment the chap arrives (it doesn't work quite so well with unwanted women), all I do is to smile and say, 'Gee, I'm glad you've come, I was about to dig a cesspit,' or something equally cheering, and in no time flat I'm on my own once again. This system is best exploited if, as the guest hurriedly leaves, I remember to shout after his car, 'Come again tomorrow, I really need the help.' Seasoned friends, and there are few enough of these, stay the course, but the rest simply vanish after the first exhausting dig. It's an infallible method and one I use when I wish to thin down my rat-hunting team to manageable proportions.

So it was the well was dug and lined with secondhand bricks I'd bought from a brewery in Burton. Ernie alone stuck the course and helped me with the well, for as I've said, I can count my friends, real friends, on one hand. For a while I bucketed water up the well like a rather messy looking Rachel waiting for suitors, except that no-one could call a deep hole made inside a tin shack the ideal place to meet the opposite sex; but that year I managed to trade my thousand gallon tank for an electric pump which didn't work until I paid an out-of-work mechanic to fix it, cutting washers out of an old shoe. ('Water'll be poisonous in contact with your shoes,' scoffed Mo.) Henceforth, for five years I'd prime the pump with water and listen to the motor scream and suck up enough water to provide almost half a bath before it packed up and refused to budge an inch until all the water had been used up.

It's funny, but when I look back on those days I was a remarkably simple person, having very little, and needing even less. 'A man is rich in proportion to what he can do without' said Thoreau, the well-

Mo.

known Concord fraud, and I really did understand him I suppose. I bought an electric blanket out of my first book royalties—my entry to a sybaritic society, I suppose, and only bought a TV (black/white flickering) when Liz came. 'Didn't buy a tele until it was too late to see Buddy Holly alive,' said Porky rather enigmatically, sounding like a thinking man's Womble. I thought at the time, *not* that I paid too much attention to a man who believes that if they keeping putting back the clock each autumn, there'll come a time when there'll be no daylight at all, which makes as much sense as some of the crap propounded by Bertrand Russell.

So it was that the well suited me just fine. I walked the three miles to the Lichfield public baths when I needed a bath—roughly three times a year—paid my 15p, bathed and walked home. Things were just fine. The public health people probably didn't approve of my water supply, but then I doubt if the public health actually approved of me anyway.

Well about ten years ago, one of the people living in the lane managed to pester the public health or water board, I've forgotten which, to put a mains water supply in the lane, cost to the householder £50 a head. My well water suited me fine so I didn't chip in the fifty quid and besides that, ten years ago I didn't have fifty pounds to spare. So I bungled on, priming my pump, replacing its worn washers every time my shoes fell apart, allowing Mo's comments of plague and typhoid to fall on deaf ears. Anyway, things took a turn for the worse for the rich mains water people in the lane that winter. In December an almighty frost gripped the district, bursting every pipe and causing the flooding of every cottage in the lane. Every cottage, nay not so. My water supply froze at well level and left me humping water from the nearby stream, breaking the ice, draining the mud but what the hell, time was the only thing of which I had plenty.

A summer of drought followed that winter of discontent, a drought which began in June and parched the ground until September. I saw sheep drink that year, a novelty, as pasture-fed sheep get enough dew and grass to keep alive. Drinking, in fact, became the death of several, for they waded into the stream opposite the cottage and got bogged down in the mud churned up alongside the fast-drying stream. I knackered three of these old ewes for my dogs, horrid bloated beasts which exploded as soon as my knife entered the viscera, giving off a strong sweet cloying smell which clung to my coat and hair, leaving even the pungent 5K avoiding me as I marked their register—the stench must have been dreadful. Fragrance and dead sheep aside, that drought changed my life in no uncertain fashion.

Each day the water in my well sank lower and lower. 'Ain't using it for bathing, that's for certain' sneered Mo contemptuously, always a bit spiteful about my lack of hygiene. . . . 'Talk about the problem yer best friends won't tell yer about—Christ, by pissing August yer won't 'ave no bleeding friends at all.' My pump gurgled ceaselessly, trying to suck up the slurry water and unpleasant mix littering the floor of the well. 'Offer the bugger a new shoe as a sacrifice,' said Ernie, 'see if it will persuade the bugger to work.' I cut up a shoe, a left-over from a tinker site, replaced the washer, but it made no difference. The gurgling sound eased a little perhaps, took on a softer note maybe, but the pump continued to suck up the thin, oily, brownish mud from the bottom of the well. I strained the filth through a muslin gauze lent to me by Mrs Harrison, our local winemaker; but while the gauze strained off most of the mud, the remaining water was dark brown and had an odd unwholesome iridescence about it, a bit like the gloss on a starling's wing. 'Sort of attractive when the light plays on it,' remarked Mo, as he ungraciously poured his tea down the drain.

So it came to pass that come hell or high water (a clever pun if you think about it) next year I'd be on the mains water, so I bred Pagan to pay the £54.15p to pay for the cost of connecting my taps to the mains water supply. Well it's taken 1,500 words to reach the point of this chapter, and we've run out of stories about cisterns, wells and mains water supplies, so the rest of the chapter is primarily about dogs.

I hadn't had a litter of puppies since Omega's mother's litter, partly because rearing puppies is a hell of a chore, but primarily because I hate having strangers to my house to buy puppies. The snooty stares of city dwellers out for a day in the country, to stare in blank disbelief at how the other half attempts to live are not so bad, but recently an advert for working terriers tends to lure in the unwholesome, seedy, long-coated, tattooed and earrings brigade, who don't really want to buy a puppy, but whose bright shiny stoat-like eyes tend to size up my pathetic little cottage for anything stealable. In fact I had to steel myself to mate Janey to Jaeger to breed a saleable litter of cross-bred working terriers in order to scratch up £54.15p to go on the mains.

Cross-breds they were for Jaeger wasn't a Jack Russell type terrier. I'd inbred to Vampire and Warlock just a little too much, I'm afraid, and began to pay the price of such an injudicious breeding programme. All sorts of physical peculiarities were beginning to manifest themselves. True, I'd bred away from the hideous and lethal cleft palates and the equally hideous and even more lethal hydrocephaly, but now some unpleasant little nuisance factors were beginning to manifest themselves. All true breeding strains carry unpleasant recessive factors which begin to appear when the breeder becomes a little over-confident and begins to inbreed to a tight little breeding nucleus. My own family of terriers were breeding very true to type at the time, all were nearly exactly the same height—about 11 inches give or take a fraction, all were blanket marked, straight legged and as game as they come. Come to think of it they were also a fairly poisonous bunch. Likewise all were beginning to show hind leg weaknesses, patella problems and narrow snipey mousey heads. Some were breeding incomplete mouths—just a few irregularly placed teeth; I'm told this defect is not unknown (magnificent understatement) in some strains of Alsatian. New blood was essential and so rather than chance using one of the chance bred Jack Russells seen at shows, dogs which could trace their ancestry back two generations to Birmingham Dogs Home, I plumped for one of those smooth-coated terriers commonly known as Patterdales.

The origin of this type of terrier is curious. I've gone into it fairly deeply in my book of fell terriers so I won't repeat myself now. Sufficient to say a pair of fell terrier breeders namely Cyril Breay and Frank Buck had set to and bred a superlative strain of fell terriers using hard coated Lakeland bred terriers quite distinct from the show bench Lakeland terriers of today. The pair had produced a strain of red or black smooth or broken coated terriers with good coats, superb heads and above all, bottomless guts, great commonsense and superb working ability. Breay had been dead for some time when I purchased Yaeger and the strain had been bastardised by mating all sorts of odds and sods ranging from pedigree Lakeland terriers to Staffordshire bull-terriers. The original stock were twelve inches tall and devoid of the bull terrier look we associate with the strain today, though strong heads were found on all of Bray's terriers. A few breeders stuck to Bray's original line: Parkes of Kirkby Overblow, Westmoreland of Troutbeck, Nuttall of Holmes Chapel and Hinchcliffe of the Pennine Hunt. I finally bought a puppy from Hinchcliffe—a red which appeared in his usually black strain and called the puppy Jaeger—which means hunter in German—and boy, did his puppies live up to their father's name.

First generation puppies got by Jaeger out of one of my own bitches would be tan or black-and-tan in colour, for tan is a dominant colour and Hinchcliffe's strain bred true to type without the odd Jack Russell type puppy appearing in the occasional litter (and a sure test of racial impurity is if a Russell type appears in a supposedly pure-bred fell terrier litter). My plan was to sell off the first generation bitches cheaply on the agreement they would be brought back to be mated with Vampire. The resultant puppies from Vampire to the half bred fell × Plummer terrier litter would be 50% tan and 50% Plummer marked and would breed true to type. I'll explain or maybe confuse things even further by using a diagram:

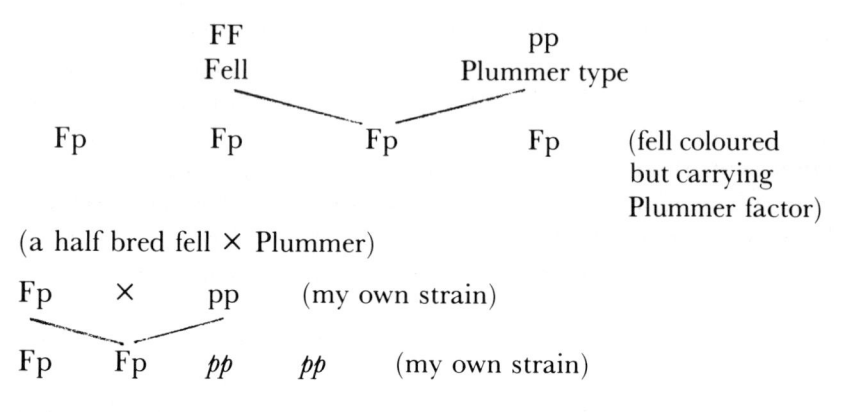

```
                    FF                      pp
                    Fell                    Plummer type

    Fp         Fp         Fp         Fp         (fell coloured
                                                but carrying
                                                Plummer factor)

(a half bred fell × Plummer)

    Fp    ×    pp              (my own strain)

    Fp    Fp    pp        pp        (my own strain)
```

Thus I hoped to give my own strain breathing space by allowing in a spot of new blood without losing the type and marking. OK, so another factor crept in unbeknown to me, a cocked ear on 50% of the puppies; but that's another story. My plan was to breed the litter, sell them on breeding terms, pay my £54.15p and get a dash of fell blood back in my own strain of Russell. The best laid plans of mice and Plummer gang aft agley (a saying I've never really understood anyway though it is repeated ad nauseam on the Moira Anderson Hogmanay Show).

Mo came down on his luck on the Monday before Janey's litter was due to be born, not an infrequent state of affairs believe me, so reluctantly I forgot my mains water for another two months and lent him Janey, promising to buy back the puppies. It sounds magnanimous, the down-at-heel teacher distributing largesse like a philanthropist with loose joints, but it isn't as it seems. Mo would have done the same for me and anyway it had rained like hell and my well was full to overflowing once again (so also was my cesspit which was dangerously and illegally near to my well). I think Ernie wisecracked about getting my own back and refused to drink the tea but that again is another story. Anyway I won £60 in a write-a-caption contest for a famous brand of detergent that week so I had the water laid on after all. Actually I submitted three captions, two unbelievably filthy ones that brought a letter of approval from the girls in the sorting room, and the third which won the prize.

Mo didn't fare so well with Janey however. She went her term and jammed in parturition, needing a Caesarian operation to get the puppies out of her, so Mo didn't gain on the deal very much, as it transpired. That's life, I guess, one minute you're down and the next down further still. It's happened to me so often that the malaise is called Plummer's syndrome by the medical profession. I hate the sort who, seeing my problems, says cherrily 'Cheer up, things could get worse'—for they usually do, mate, they usually do. Three puppies came from the Caesarian section, a bitch which went to Miller, an elderly retired railway worker who works as a part-timer terrier man for a hunt some miles from Derby, Toby, Mick Kirby's useful terrier and the third, a black-and-tan bitch I bought back from Mo and called Pagan.

Somehow or the other and experts call it hybrid vigour, two strains of inbred animal mated together produce offspring which not only have the best qualities of both parents but a few qualities which neither parents possessed. Janey was a useful hunter, a good hunter killer combination but no great shakes, I must admit; while Jaeger was a nervy dog, apprehensive enough to make him little use as a competitive rat-killing dog, for a first rate rat dog must act first and think later. Neither parent was a top-grade rat terrier yet Miller's bitch, Toby and Pagan have to be seen to be believed. Even as babes they were furious little creatures, willing and more than able to take on most things and such was their nerve, their *élan vital*, that they had to be separated before they were eight weeks old as the three were in danger of becoming two, or maybe even one. Toby became one of those instant terriers, dogs which go for any quarry without having to be entered. He found a dead badger when he was six months and had to be choked off it. Miller's bitch became a famous hunter, a wonderful ratter and a great bolter and an all round heller, a bit mousey-headed perhaps but none the worse for that. Pagan became the second-best rat dog I've ever owned and having said that I must mention she damned nigh did for the best I've ever owned.

Pagan entered early, killing her first rat around a farm in Atherstone. It was an unfair kill I suppose as Pagan surprised a cat which had trapped a rat behind a water barrel, dabbing it with her paws until fear and maybe a few judicious clawings had reduced it to near death. Still, it bolted and, when Pagan ran forward and picked it up, it came out of its near-catatonic state and retaliated with a sharp bite or so. Pagan was fifteen weeks old at the time with milk teeth and unable to kill the rat cleanly. She dropped it as though it was red hot, shook her head to clear the sting of the bite and then went berserk. An hour later after I had drunk my tea, eaten my usual piece of sticky, stomach-murdering fruit cake, I left the farmhouse to find Pagan still shaking hell out of the rat, her eyes blazing and her heart pounding like a drum. An idiot would have realised that, despite her colour, she would be a treasure in the team.

Pagan lived up to her early promise a hundredfold and became one of the best all round catcher/hunter bitches in the pack. Her nose was extraordinary, her immunity to pain almost alarming (and a rat hunt, a proper rat hunt, not a mosey around Dad's garden shed, really tests a dog's mettle). Her catching ability took some beating as well; and though she lacked Omega's ability to be exactly at the right place at the right time, I've never seen a bitch 'as all round useful' as Pagan. Normally a rat pack enters the lists as a general free-for-all, all dogs hunting and all dogs killing, but if a pack is to succeed, the terriers sort themselves out as predominantly killers and predominantly hunters. This doesn't mean to say that no catch dog will hunt or that no nose terrier will catch. The best packs are made up of dogs which quickly polarise to the extremes. Pagan was a good nose dog and also a good catch dog. Omega was simply an outstanding catch dog. Kali and Teen, two of Beltane's super daughters, were strictly hunters, prepared to work the trays until they dropped, though not particularly dextrous at killing large rats quickly. Phobos, the bandy-legged son of Vampire and Beltane, a dog which looks like Bambi and acts like a psychopath, is a dual purpose dog, and like Teen will give tongue like thunder when a rat is just out of reach in a cage. Unlike Teen, he is also an incredible rat killer, who once spiked his face when he leaped into a harrow after an escaping rat. The harrow tine went clean through his cheeks and gums, leaving a hole as wide as a pencil; but he never murmured when it happened, hunting the evening as though he was unhurt and only when crating him to take him home did I realise the extent of his injuries. Such catch-and-hunt dogs are rare in a pack,

Pagan catches at an incredible angle.

as I've explained; and a good job too, for to be an efficient unit, a pack needs to be polarised.

Kennelling terriers is always a problem, and though I have what might be classed by some as unlimited space (an acre and a quarter to be exact), when things get hectic, where to put the dogs and with whom is a bit of a problem. Dogs usually kennel well with bitches. Admittedly my border terrier dog will attack and bowl any bitch put in with him, snarling like a lion and menacing the bitch like a fiend. However, an hour later he'll be cleaning her and fawning like a fool. Vampire is difficult to kennel with either a bitch or dog (God forbid kennelling him with a dog). Some bitches he will accept, others he attacks as soon as they come near him. I usually kennel him with his geriatric older sister Beltane, who accepts his crotchety bad-tempered ways stoically, and spends her days licking and cleaning his battered face.

Omega is easy to kennel with dog or bitch; or at least she used to be and for a while I kennelled her with Pagan. Skirmishes did occur, I must admit, but skirmishes between terrier bitches are things one accepts within a pack and they usually cause no harm. The really deadly vendetta, the evil hatred between the two started as a result of a curious event.

Certain actions, places, smells, trigger off memories for me. I hate launderettes, not (as Moses believes) because of my lack of personal hygiene, but quite simply because the smell of soap powder triggers off unpleasant memories. I'll explain. I ran away from home when I was sixteen—an action which upset Mam quite a bit for she started looking for me when I was thirty-four—and literally bummed around Europe like a juvenile and dishevelled W. H. Davies. Behind one of the market places in Paris is a huge pile of cardboard boxes, which are collected every fortnight, and once when I was on the road and down on my luck I lived for four days in one of these huge detergent boxes. It was a pleasant enough place to live, cramped I admit; and smelling strongly of soap powder. It was also fairly unpleasant when it rained and a bit frothy as well. Many winoes lived in neighbouring boxes, friendly enough chaps of all nationalities, willing to exchange a swig of Bluey (a mix of lemonade and meths which ate away my plastic anorak) for a sandwich or so, but my sojourn among the boxes came to an unpleasant end when I returned home to my box one Thursday to

Omega

find the dustbin men had moved my box together with my rucksack which I'd found in Calais. Hence my antipathy for launderettes; and, come to think of it, I'm none too partial to French refuse collectors either. I told this story to my doctor a few days back, and he wrote something beginning with 'psy' on his pad, but that's another story.

Omega's antipathy to Pagan was sparked off by something equally curious. I think I've mentioned Petheridge, a prince among berks, and for a while I thought he'd gone out of my life for ever. Well it seems I wasn't that lucky for like the proverbial bad penny, Petheridge always seems to turn up. As I've mentioned, I have a fair patch of land with my shack, weedy, wet, but place enough for kennels and usually I have a few kennels to spare. Well, Petheridge turned up at my cottage one evening while I was feeding my dogs. 'How much do you pay for tripes, Bri?' I told him. He fell back in amazement at my weekly expenditure. 'Yer don't 'ave one to spare?', a strange request as he didn't own a dog, but Petheridge with a nose for the free (and one doesn't need much of a nose to detect tripe), sensed he could sell it to someone at a profit. I put him off gently, mentally dealing him a Nagasaki death chop or a Cleveland back breaker as he turned. God, I hate Petheridge, his eternal scrounging, his nose for money making schemes which do not involve his sweat but mine. Basically, Petheridge is a miser, a mean, stingy, pathetic sickening miser, the sort of man who, if he had two perforated gastric ulcers, would be reluctant to part with one unless the price was right. There is a story amongst my friends that Petheridge asks his barber to return Petheridge's hair clippings, but such a tale is probably libellous, as my friends also find Petheridge hard to stomach. I wish that I could come out with some of the caustic Denis Norden type quips whenever Petheridge appears, but I can only think of something clever to say days after Petheridge had gone. Petheridge got to the point of his visit fairly quickly, that is, after he had ascertained that I wouldn't give him some fencing posts, twenty yards of chain linked fencing, some galvanised sheets and my entire crop of gooseberries—'There's an old age pensioner who lives near me Bri and she loves gooseberries. Yer don't know where I could get a really good, really good' he added, to emphasise his point—'Jack Russell puppy.' A few weeks before he had seen a very pregnant bitch in the run no doubt. 'Reasonable like, reasonable price.' (Petheridge had a sale for such a pup no doubt.) 'It's for?', I waited, knowing what would come, 'an old age pensioner.' Either Petheridge is a liar or else the pensioners around his place are over-energetic fiends who enjoy bull baiting and stock car racing. Last year Petheridge had asked for 'a nice little terrier "doing a bit" for an old man who wants to try a spot of badger digging'. (You lie Petheridge, you lie.) 'Yer, a nice little good quality Jack Russell, reasonable like,' he continued. I shook my head concerning his having one of my puppies, and closing my eyes I saw a large creature known only in Celtic legends, devouring Petheridge, whose left leg protruded from the beast's mouth while Petheridge's head, deep inside the beast's cavernous gullet continued to bleat about the scandalous price of admission. A smile creased my lips as Petheridge muttered, 'Bleeding mad you are, smiling at nothing. D'yer know anyone with puppies?' I mentioned Death Wish Muldoon, a suicidal Irishman from this side of Derby, a lunatic well known at the casualty hospital for his interest in ending it all. Death Wish is a rotten dog breeder and not all that good at suicide either, for he is still with us. Yes, Death Wish had puppies, stacks of them, all badly reared, all checked in growth through Death Wish's weekly stints at the psychiatrist and mental institution. I mentioned Death Wish and told Petheridge the price. It was as if I'd hit Petheridge between the eyes with a hammer. 'How much, Christ I never expected to pay as much as six pounds' (the going price for decent puppies at that time was about £25). I closed my eyes once more and launched a deadly Exocet missile tipped with curare at Petheridge, blowing him into a thousand bleating miserly little pieces. 'Christ, I'm not a tight wad, but six quid.' He was visibly reeling at the suggestion of coughing up six measly pounds for one of Death Wish's puppies. Six quid, scarcely enough to keep Death Wish in Valium for a week.

   I didn't see Petheridge for a month or so afterwards and it was well into June before he appeared with a scruffy, ugly Russell bitch with prick ears and a pig mouth, peering out of the back of his car. Why have you come, Petheridge, I asked myself mentally, treating him to a quick machine gunning for good measure. He jumped out of his car, cocky as ever, 'Got her for nothing at the dog pound, ain't paying six bleeding pounds,' he sneered. The bitch lifted her lips as Petheridge waved his arms, leaping at the windows to show her hatred of Petheridge. I fell in love with her instantly, warmed to her when I saw we shared at least something in common. 'A bit touchy actually,' Petheridge went on. I touched the window and she leaped, teeth bared at me, thereby ending our love affair. 'What I really wanted,' Petheridge continued, getting to the meat of his reason for his visit, 'is to ask a favour.' No, no, Petheridge, my mind screamed, sod off, get lost, go take a running jump at yourself free, here's a bob for the gas meter, use it wisely. Here's two in case a bob isn't enough to see you off, but all I could manage to stutter was 'Yes, how can I help?' I hated myself for being such a coward. 'D'yer know how much the bleeding boarding kennels want for taking the bitch for a week? Christ, it's not as if she's a pedigree or summat, after all I didn't have to pay for her.' Petheridge was off on a cut price holiday in the Costa Del something or other, a holiday when he would treat his anaemic wife and kids to bruised fruit and tainted meat, knowing the water would give them Spanish tummy but hoping they'd be able to stick it out until they arrived back home in England where medical treatment is free.

I'm always a bit careful about dogs which finish up at a dogs' home, not because they're actually from a dogs' home, but because their owners haven't bothered to claim them. If one of my dogs gets lost I go frantic, phoning the police, asking around and visiting every dogs' home from here to Tewkesbury. I admit there are callous swine who lose interest in dogs and let them remain in an Animal Refuge (a curious name for a place where they electrocute stray dogs), but some dogs finish up in such places simply because they are barmy. It's common practice today for social workers (who I believe are the modern day equivalent of the plagues which struck Egypt) to defend a thug who had just 'done' for an old woman by stating that no wonder he was depraved, he grew up in a 'home', as if the 'home' was responsible for the little sod's vicious streak. The chances are that if one checked back far enough in the child's history, one would find a host of stricken guinea pigs, eviscerated hamsters and wingless flies that he'd put to the sword before he eventually went into the 'home', and that the only reason that he had no parents was that he's killed his mother and father to go to the orphans' tea party. Likewise dogs and Animal Shelters. Some owners probably breathe a sigh of relief when their beloved dogs just don't turn up. Such was the case with Petheridge's Russell.

The bitch had all the makings of the ideal pet for the Petheridge household—mean, spiteful with a decidedly sly, treacherous streak. Admittedly she'd nailed Petheridge through his legs a few times which shows she wasn't all bad, but as soon as she arrived she'd set about me in the same manner, eventually backing into her kennel, squealing and wetting herself when I approached her, putting bite after bite into my gently proferred hand. After a week on my premises I could easily understand why her original owner had let her remain in a dogs' home. Omega and Pagan took an instant dislike to the bitch which threw itself at the bars of her kennels, lips lifted and teeth bared when the pair even sniffed her shed. Both wagged their tails in a most amazingly unconcerned manner when she performed like this, and had I been half the stockman my vanity allows me to believe I am, I would have interpreted the tail wagging of both Omega and Pagan differently and realised the shape of things to come. As it was I was only too grateful to be able to slip the swine's food into her without getting badly bitten. Pagan and Omega had taken a dislike to the Petheridge bitch which was called Patch, Queenie or some equally imaginative name.

I'm a lousy carpenter, and when I build a set of kennels—which is quite a frequent event as my dogs are destructive to wooden kennels—the doors rarely fit properly. Hence my dogs get out all too frequently and I invariably arrive home to find two or maybe more terriers in the porch. Well, to get to the essence of the tale, I awoke one morning to a screaming and roaring from the run. If a terrier man lives as closely to his dogs as I do, the barking of terriers becomes a separate language of its own and every murmur, whimper or scream can be easily translated. Beltane's high-pitched yodelling late at night means she has heard a rat in the hedgerow. Vampire's strangled cry of rage means a rival male is in the run and is micturating over Vampire's marking post. Sadly, Pagan's sobbing roar now means that Omega is out in the run, but before the day in question they kennelled together quite happily.

I rose, slipped on my shoes and raced out to the run for the battle cry meant something serious was amiss. Omega and Pagan were out, but what was worse was that both had jumped against the door of Petheridge's bitch's pen so forcefully that the door had sprung open and by the time I had managed to get in the run the unholy alliance were well on their way to killing Petheridge's bitch.

Dog fights are curious ritualistic affairs and I'm fairly convinced Jack London never owned a dog let alone witnessed a ritual battle; and all dog fights, save the combat between two enraged pit bull terriers, are rituals. A one to one fight, a duel between two reasonably well matched antagonists rarely ends in a death. Admittedly, there is a story of early Bedlington terriers, the appraisal of whose courage reads, 'When two meet only one walks away,' but this, like many other tales of the borders, must be taken with a pinch of salt. Face to face or throat to throat battles are really games of bluff and once superiority has been established, the vanquished remains underneath the victor until the top dog decides to allow the underdog to walk away. When the fight becomes a three-way battle the contest takes on a far more sinister nature.

Three-way battles, particularly battles between adolescent bitches, youngsters which still have hypodermic sharp milk teeth but are feeling the cockiness of approaching adulthood, are very nasty. One dog will lock to the face of another while the third wreaks havoc between the legs of the loser, ripping, tearing or worse still plucking at the bowels and muscles of the hindlegs. Gog, Rollo's daughter, was mauled by such a fight a few months ago and carries a permanently crippled hindleg as a souvenir of the battle. Balan, a son of Twirl, Rupert's copper, red and white son, was gelded by just such a battle one Sunday when a rabbit turned back into the mêlée of terriers and triggered off one of the worst fights I've ever seen. Two-way fights don't worry me and I usually let them finish rather than chance another battle taking place next exercise period. Vampire is an exception, I admit, and he continues on long after the battle should have ceased; but Vampire, I believe, has a tile loose and doesn't conform to rules.

Omega and Pagan were really killing Petheridge's bitch by the time I pushed the gate open and ran up the exercise enclosure. Omega was locked face to face with her and Pagan wreaking havoc between the hindlegs. As I raced up the run, kicking, hitting and swearing at the antagonists, I saw Omega prepare to leave the battle to escape my wrath, but as she released her hold Petheridge's bitch in agony caused by the damage Pagan was inflicting, struck at Omega. The battle took on a bizarre appearance as Omega suddenly turned and struck at Pagan, maybe believing that the painful bite across her eyes had not come from Petheridge's stricken beast, but from Pagan. Whatever the reason, and I doubt if dogs embroiled in battle have reasons, I believe that split second determined the future of both Pagan and Omega. They dropped Petheridge's monstrosity and set about each other like fiends, rolling, throwing each other, covering each other with saliva and the filth which had flooded out of their victim. I left them and grabbed Petheridge's bitch who in terror put a neat set of punctures through my right hand, snapping a bone on her way through my hand. I fenced with her snapping mouth, tailed her and put her under the heat lamp and phoned my vet. Only then did I return to the

A bitter resentment had developed between Pagan and Omega.

antagonists who were going at each other hell for leather while Vampire watched the contest from his pen, saliva dripping from his lop-sided face, his eyes glazed with ecstasy.

   To separate two battlers is an easy task, nasty but not particularly difficult (though it would draw a wince from an RSPCA official), but the seeds of hatred between the two had been planted during that ridiculous fight. Earlier that morning they had been curled up asleep together; now they leapt at the bars of their cages to get to each other, screaming hatred and their teeth bared like strange prehistoric carnivores.

   There are two ways of settling such vendettas; and I get quite a lot of petty kennel bickering, so I'm reasonably adept at sorting out their canine social problems. Putting them together to sort out their dispute was a bit out of the question. For a day or two the antagonists would literally bite eight bells out of each other before a pecking order was established after which sweetness and light may not prevail, but at least one or the other would gain respect of the victor and things would settle down once more. However at that time we were hunting four nights a week and I could not afford both my best dogs being out of action. Furthermore, Omega's unbeaten record had attacted hosts of punters, each one prepared to put £100 or so on so and so's Queenie etc. Omega had five straight easy contests lined up over the next month, so a limping bitch with a torn mouth, frayed ears and sundry other damage was not exactly what I wanted. I'd had a nutter phone that week, a man who was prepared to match his six month old American Pit Bull terrier, a floppy 60 lb brute against Omega at ratting and prepared to stake, as he put it, £500 where his mouth was! Well so much for money and mouth, for I never heard from him again.

The other alternative was to keep the pair entirely separate and hope that they'd forget their little vendetta. This, too, was difficult for, as I've explained, I was doing four nights a week at David's. While I was pretty certain that during the hectic hunting first time around the sheds, both Omega and Pagan would be too preoccupied with the rats to concern themselves with fighting, once we hit a lull in the hunting while we waited for the next shift of rats to come out and feed, the antagonists would suddenly remember their little differences. Furthermore, there is no way a terrier man can keep the rest of the pack from joining in the mêlée once two terriers start to skirmish with each other. Separating the pair seemed the best method of containing the situation, though in the light of what was to follow, perhaps allowing the pair to sort out their differences in one hellish two-way battle would have been best.

Meanwhile back at the ranch, Petheridge's bitch looked far from well. She was hideously lacerated, badly bruised and had several small bones broken. Furthermore it took me nearly an hour to duck and dodge her snaps and bites and pin her down for the vet to examine her. Omega's and Pagan's attentions hadn't exactly helped the bitch's paranoid disposition, believe me. My vet and I engaged in a very dextrous sleight of hand, and finally managed to bundle the screaming animal into the van and take her to the surgery for intensive care treatment, a little venture which cost me £70 in hard-earned cash.

Petheridge arrived next day for his bitch, a suntan darkening his normally deathly white face. I told him about the bitch, watching his anaemic wife attempting to force a few tears which made her mascara run until she looked like a raccoon. I explained about the damage, told Petheridge I'd pay and offered £10 compensation. Another burst of tears from Mrs P. upped the price of my guilt to £20 and ten minutes later Petheridge accepted £100 for the trouble I'd caused him! As he left, he commented rather tartly, 'We'll leave her at a boarding kennels next year, Clarice, it's safer.' Safer, maybe, Petheridge, but scarcely as rewarding, I'll bet.

I fielded a good team that night, still fuming over Petheridge's nerve and miserly nature, vowing to commit mayhem if he was foolish enough to visit my place again. I loaded Vampire, Beltane, Pagan my border terrier, Omega, Phoibos and Demos into the trailer and set out for David's place, vowing to have the hunt to end all hunts to make me forget the little wizened extortionist who was probably sitting at home planning how to screw another £100 out of me.

We had a superb evening's sport, fast, furious and fairly productive, that is for a July night when most self-respecting rats are living it up in some hedgerow or other rather than feeding in a foetid, steaming hot poultry pen. Omega didn't even look at Pagan and even Phoibos and Demos who were determined to see off their sire Vampire, were impeccably behaved—until the hedgehog incident, that is.

Frankly, hedgehogs are the bane of my life and responsible for more 'at exercise' fights and deaths than I care to mention. Not that hedgehogs are ferocious beasts; far from it, in fact, though I did receive a hell of a bite from one while hunting a played-out allotment when I was maybe twelve years old. It is the fact that hedgehogs are innocuous creatures which causes me trouble. When attacked, troubled, bewildered or maybe just when they wish to be a bit cussed, a hedgehog simply rolls into a ball and waits, rather like a director of education or a chief constable of police. This method of defence works fine against stoats, hawks and owls (or in the case of a chief constable an irate member of the public), though it does come amiss against motor vehicles, as the number of spiney splats up and down the motorway attests.

Dogs meeting this seemingly inert little bundle of spines react according to their nature. Most rush up to the beast, circle it, attempting to bite into the spines and then, realising that this is going to hurt them rather than the hedgehog, begin to bark frantically at the apparently ill-constructed ball of prickles. Vampire simply rushes up, sees the hedgehog, noses it over and bites straight into the spines killing the poor wretch and causing himself a whole load of distress and me another bundle of vet's bills. Come to think of it, it might have been better if Vampire had come on the damned hedgehog first.

As it was, Beltane did, and Beltane, always the sane and calm one of my team, began to nose the beast over, barking softly as she did so.

Omega, attracted by the noise, ran up and began to maul the bundle of spines, barking shrilly. Pagan joined the pair, barking as she did so and the howls suddenly went up. One moment, each dog fascinated with the hedgehog, the next a raging five-way battle was taking place with Omega locked into Pagan's face, Beltane harrying the flanks and Phoibos and Demos had, for no reason other than that it seemed like a good idea at the time, pitched into Vampire—not a sensible action as they were later to discover, but then Phoibos and Demos are not exactly famous for their common sense.

I ran in clubbing, kicking, dragging and throwing water over the battlers, finally flinging Beltane twelve feet up into a meal bunker and hurling Vampire after her. Phoibos and Demos, now elated by Vampire's aerial departure, set about Pagan with a vengeance—and boy, do I mean with a vengeance. I've never timed a fight—they all seem like an eternity though I try to end them quickly—but the battle took on gargantuan proportions resembling a Cecil B. DeMille film rather than a skirmish. Finally, I separated the battlers after Pagan's jaw had been smashed like matchwood. Phoibos and Demos were torn quite badly and Omega boasted a solitary puncture below her jaws. Above me, in the hopper, Beltane was screaming blue murder as

A desperate fight between Pagan and Omega about to begin.

Vampire, now made ecstatic by the sound of combat, set about her like a fiend.

Roughly speaking, and very roughly at that, there are three types of bite inflicted in a dog fight. Firstly, the chopping slash which usually precedes every major battle, a bite usually put in with the speed of a piston. Such bites are long, narrow and often bleed copiously, and for a day or two after the battle look deceptively dangerous and nasty. The second type of bite is the skin and flesh crushing bite put in by a dog with bull-terrier blood, a bite which crushes and macerates the blood vessels and surrounding flesh. Often these bites heal as black leathery scars, though if the dog is well and not prone to dying of shock (and many dogs die of shock after receiving such bites) these flesh-mangling bites heal very well. Thirdly there is the deep puncture, a bite which spikes through tissue, causing little bleeding, no tissue mangling, and a hell of a lot of canine deaths.

If one of my males is spiked, I clean the wound as best I can and kennel him with Beltane, who is an ardent cleaner of wounds on other dogs—not because of any Florence Nightingale instinct, I feel I should add, but simply because Beltane enjoys licking something decidedly necrotic: a disgusting habit it may be, but one which has its uses, as dog saliva contains a powerful antiseptic called lysozyme. (I didn't teach biology for nothing!) By now, however, the friction between Omega, Pagan and Beltane was such that to kennel any two would be courting disaster.

True to form, the wound went wrong and a huge abscess formed below Omega's jaw, making her look like one of those thyroid cases suffering from a malady called Derbyshire Neck. I wasn't particularly worried at first. I'd seen abscesses form and burst time without number and they'd healed up quite nicely. The contents of an abscess is nasty, but apparently completely sterile, so the sight of an enormous goitre on a terrier's throat shouldn't cause the terrier keeper too much concern. Omega looked decidedly unhappy, but three weeks later the abscess burst and we were back on the road again, ratting three nights a week as if nothing had happened—except that the hideous abscess began to fill up again and this time Omega began to lose weight drastically.

I believe in modern medicine, antiseptics, antibiotics and all that jazz, and while I'm a bit against the 'cure it by Valium' cult, I'm aware that life has been a whole lot easier since Lister came up with antiseptics, and Fleming 'made it' by growing something nasty in bowls of sugary liquid. I tried every damned thing I know on Omega's abscess, desperately putting off the machos who insisted my bitch competed against their world-beating dogs, but penicillin and sundry other strange-sounding antibiotics had no effect. There didn't seem a lot of point cleaning out the wound with ordinary antiseptics, but as I continued to experiment with all and sundry, Omega looked worse and worse as the abscess became bigger and bigger.

A word of advice, now, reader: if you dislike the gory, the horrendous, if you literally turn pale at House of Usher type stuff, skip the rest of the chapter, for the next few paragraphs should have one of those little squares one sees on TV shows when the next bit is unsuitable for children or adults for that matter—the sort of squares that cause a battle royal once the kids realise that something nasty is coming on the screen and you want them out of the room.

I suppose I have some strange friends by any standards. Death Wish with his morbid preoccupation with the hereafter doesn't exactly qualify for the title Mr Average, neither does Ernie, a villainous looking ruffian from our local cafe who boasts that he killed a man with a karate blow to the 'jubbly', whatever that is. Peewee Mcgurk has cementy grained hands, Love and Hate tattooed on his knuckles, and a blue bird fluttering its way up his thumb, which is tastefully labelled 'Sid'; and though he claims to be an accountant, I don't think I would trust my accounts to anyone who calls his thumb 'Sid'. Furthermore, I do not like Peewee very much, particularly since he became involved in a rather nasty little incident in The Rose Bowl and bit off a fellow drunkard's thumb. Peewee has a thing about thumbs. Indeed there must be some extraordinary people in the Institute of Chartered Accountants, and some old ladies wishing to invest £500 on gilt-edged securities will be in for a very bad time if they contradicted Peewee!

Peewee, Death Wish and the jubbly-chopping Ernie from the cafe can't hold a candle to Paul Chance, however, an academic, a PhD and now lecturer in an American university who at one time said, 'To hell with it all,' gave up his job, married a fashion designer and went on his honeymoon in a hearse, thereby inviting a host of what I considered very funny but unrepeatable comments from Mo, but it isn't the honeymoon by hearse which causes me to regard Paul as strange. What fascinates me about him is that, in spite of his education, he has earthy and downright primitive ideas about medicine, food and life in general. Paul has teeth extracted without an anaesthetic, whereas I need an anaesthetic to get me to the dentist. Paul stitches not only the rips in his running dogs, but also his own wounds on his arms, legs and chest. Still, he looks amazingly well on his strange diet, his interest in needlework and earthy way of life, which is curious for the most desperately ill looking people I've ever seen seem to be working in health shops.

Back once again to the plot—and the nasty bit. Paul arrived late that August and watched Omega looking pitiful in her kennels, her neck almost hanging with this enormous goitre just ready to burst and the necrotic wound in her neck black with blow flies. 'I'd let those hatch, if I were you,' said Paul, inspecting the blow fly eggs laid in the wound. I'd seen Paul clean up a very bad wound using maggots; and now, with antibiotics not exactly working and antiseptics a little bit short of the art, I was reaching for straws. Omega weighed less than ten pounds, ten pounds of lacklustre fur and emaciated frame, and only that filthy abscess seemed to be doing well and thriving. Reluctantly, I left the wound to its own devices and ceased to mop it with antiseptic solutions each day. The lump continued to grow until one day I went to feed her to find her lying on her side panting with the excruciating pain which accompanies the bursting of a huge abscess. A mass of filth and blood ran down her chest dappling and staining her white front. 'Don't clean it, leave it you berk,' said Paul insistently and next day I found her with blow fly maggots cleaning out the huge cavity in her neck. Twice I choked back the nausea when I went to see her, and twice nearly weakened and cleaned the huge evil-smelling hole in her neck when maggots moved in and out of a foul smelling yellow slime. 'They'll lock you up, you know,' hissed Mo, 'bleeding hell, you're nuts, both of you!' But three days later the wound had closed, the swelling vanished and a sparkle was coming back in Omega's coat. She looked very thin and emaciated and it took many months for her to recover completely. Summer, an Indian Summer at that, came, baking the stone wall near my cottage and causing the two-leaved groundsel to seed to continue the species. Plants and animals in desperate plight seem to be very fertile to ensure that the next generation will be produced to continue the species. Still it was with considerable surprise when a month or so later I found the very weak and ailing Omega in pup. What was even more surprising was how she came to be mated, and more curious still, which dog had fathered her litter.

Misalliance

At the time of writing, and God knows what tomorrow will bring in my accident prone life, I have three of Omega's offspring in my kennels, or the set of ill-constructed sheds I choose to call kennels. Rollo is her oldest puppy, an obese brute, with a bull terrier head and a tendency to get fat on scraps of food which would reduce a rat to a living skeleton. Rollo is a son of Alan Thomas's Hamish, a great and well-used badger terrier, a gentle dog, slow to anger and sensible as they come. Rollo seems to have inherited his father's peaceable disposition though sooner or later a fight with Vampire will see one or the other off, I fear. Kotian and Ilana (great names, one was an Avar chieftain, the other means a branch in Hebrew) are the other two, offspring of Forsyth's Pip, a dog I bought partly because of his shape, looks and courage and partly because of the fact that Pip's grand-

Rollo.

mother was Graham Ward's Penny, a long-dead old grappler bred from Clown and my old veteran San. Kotian and Ilana are not of the same mould as Rollo; both are spidery thin puppies at fourteen weeks of age. Kotian, the male, will thicken considerably if he lives that long, for he has a spiteful streak and last week Fat Boy (an unpretentious nickname, though he is registered as Warlock II) thrashed him within an inch of his life after he had annoyed, menaced and irritated Fat Boy beyond endurance. Ilana is the only pattern-marked bitch puppy Omega has bred, a dark coppery-red bitch more sensible than her brother, but with the bright-eyed look of her mother, the look that says, 'I'm ready for action—just try me.' The name Ilana?—it means a branch and through her the new and future bloodlines will be bred, and that is counting one's chickens before they are hatched if ever I did so! Omega bred one other litter—though we don't usually talk about that, as not only does it show stupidity on my part but also bad management, crass incompetence and a bit more besides. However, it's an interesting story, so here goes.

Omega is a curious-looking animal at times for she can drink enormous quantities of water, eat almost impossible amounts of food, swell up like a balloon and twelve hours later she is back to normal. To allow her access to food or water before a money-making competition is begging for trouble, as she can eat and drink herself into a state of stupor. What is more important to me is that Omega doesn't show colour, which to a non-dog-breeder means that she doesn't show the onset of season and does in fact come in season when she pretty well wants to; so if I intend to breed from her I need to kennel her with her chosen mate for three parts of the year.

Nothing seems to go right in my mishap-ridden life, partly because I happen to be one of those people the gods seem to have frowned on but mostly, I admit, because I am untidy, slap happy and frequently a bit dirty. Strange and weird events seem to dog me, however. Only last week an advert appeared in our local newspaper—a humdrum little rag whose leading article each and every week seems to be 'Angry councillor walks out of meeting concerning old age pensioner living in damp house'. Last week it was brightened up a little by the advert which read 'Good quality Jack Russell puppy sired by D. B. Plummer'—which I profoundly hope will be regarded as a misprint by the general public, or I can expect a visit from the vice squad or someone doing a thesis on quaint mammalian sexual behaviour. But this month has been fairly quiet as far as 'curious event' goes, at least compared to the month starting with the date when Omega's wound finally began to heal.

It began amazingly enough with Porky hammering on my front door at 3 a.m. on a Saturday morning. Breathlessly he began to explain he'd been picked up driving an untaxed, uninsured 30 cwt van and wished to borrow my insurance for my tiny 126 Fiat to show to the police. I tried desperately to explain to Porky, who stood there slavering like an upset mastiff, that my insurance didn't cover his van, but he kept repeating 'They won't notice the difference, they don't check all that careful.' Eventually in desperation he kicked my door and stormed off shouting 'You pissin' gerenuk!' I closed the door and checked up the meaning of the word gerenuk. It meant a small African antelope. I checked through Websters for an alternative meaning, but I was stuck with the African antelope. Funnily enough, I was still thinking about Porky shouting 'pissin' gerenuk' when I drove into Birmingham, and with my mind half on the road and half on the antelope I drove my mucky little Fiat smack bang into a Panda car. Thus began the disastrous month in question, and frankly the fact that a fat near-imbecile had disturbed my concentration by calling me a small African antelope didn't look all that good in a magistrate's court. On *Call My Bluff* maybe, but in a magistrate's court—no way.

Things went really awry at home. Merle, my lurcher, had taken a terrible pasting from foxes and was recuperating under a heat lamp. David had an outbreak of a mysterious disease called parvo virus at his place, and the thought of infecting my dogs with the bug nearly drove me out of my mind. Omega was greyhound thin, with sunken eyes, an odd dehydrated look and a thin, staring coat. The wound under her throat had healed to a thin, dark scar, but constitutionally she was far from right.

Things were bad in the run, but that was nothing new for things are always bad in the run. Maybe the scent of Omega's approaching season had something to do with it—I'd be a fool to hazard a guess—but Vampire was even more morose and aggressive than usual, strutting about like a pompous little man challenging the world to disagree with him. Few bitches dared to, and most hid under the shed as he roared past, lips raised, heading straight for Warlock's shed where he continued to jump at the door to settle a long overdue account, while Warlock didn't help matters much by leaping at the inside of the door to get at Vampire, who was both his brother and his mortal enemy. It was a bit like an irresistible force meeting an

A very rotund Omega. I had doubts as to the sire of the litter she was carrying.

immovable object; neither would give in, both had literally bottomless reserves of courage and what was worse, both were skilled battlers, fighters whose blind courage was garnished with the skills both had picked up during a hundred or more battles with dogs and wild quarry. Neither could be exercised while the other was out of kennels and sooner or later it was inevitable that something would occur which would trigger off the most fearsome of battles. Oddly enough, I didn't witness the decisive encounter. If I had, I would have prevented the battle or at least tried to prevent it, for it takes a pretty courageous man to get in the middle of a fight between Vampire and a victim.

I can remember arriving home from school the day of the battle and noticing the deathly silence which prevailed in the run. I'm peculiar, I suppose, but I rev up my noisy engine as I park my car just to hear my dogs bark; possibly because after a day's failure at school, any group of beasts which welcome me makes me feel great. Silence is unusual, damned unusual, for usually the din is cacophanous. The day in question, the pack remained silent even though I revved up my car until its lawnmower sized engine was literally roaring. Something was obviously wrong, and I raced into the run to find the cause of the silence. The dogs were exhausted for they had been leaping against their shed doors all day, and many pens showed the marks of teeth. The cause of their excitement and subsequent exhaustion became obvious as I walked up the run.

Vampire was loose and he literally crawled out from beneath his pen, wagging his tail feebly as he came. He looked dreadful, as though someone had thrown him against a circular saw or had been the victim of an accident with a harrow. He tottered towards me, fell, rose again weakly and stood there swaying like a dead fly in a spider's web. The cause of his condition became obvious when I looked further up the run. Warlock lay there very dead amidst a pool of blood, his mouth ajar, his eyes glazed and speckled with flecks of dust, his kennel now vacant. Warlock had managed to force his cage and leaped against Vampire's kennel repeatedly until his old antagonist had escaped. I had considered the pair equally matched, Warlock's extra size matched by Vampire's speed and unbelievable ferocity. Now watching Vampire tottering and swaying I realised I had been right. They had been almost equally matched. It had been an epic struggle, a battle where no points decision could have decided the outcome of the fight, and judging from Vampire's condition, I estimated the fight had been damned nigh a draw. I didn't bother to bury Warlock until I had hastily threw a sack around Vampire and put him under a heat lamp far from the equally damaged Merle. He was bleeding from a dozen bites and his throat was a macerated pulp through which cords of muscle pulsed and quivered. I have never seen a dog so badly lacerated and I held out little hope of recovery. At that moment in time a visit from the RSPCA would have closed my premises and the *News of the World* would have carried an article which would probably have read 'The monster who taught children'. The inmates of my kennel looked awful. Merle was desperately ill and emaciated. Warlock was dead, his body gruesomely torn, Vampire was so lacerated that my vet advised me to put him down and Omega was skeleton-thin, her once glossy coat looking dull and lifeless.

Still, things carry on in spite of losses. After the distemper outbreak which saw off Jade's litter mates, after the loss of Tuffy and Stealer, after the death of San, I felt like packing it up, jacking in dogs and life for good. Now once more the depression struck again. Winter was on me again and the very cold of my ill-made cottage caused my depression to deepen. I contemplated resigning, getting out of teaching, selling my shack for the pittance it was worth, and hightailing it north to Scotland, where no doubt another failure awaited me. It's times like this when I realise the insularity of my lonely existence, but such moods seldom last and the pendulum once again swings to the manic side of the manic/depressive cycle. Within days Vampire had started to stand up, Merle had begun to gain weight and Omega had begun to flesh out until she looked quite plump. Too plump in fact, and after a week or so of hunting it became obvious to all and sundry that she was either suffering from a type of bloat unknown to veterinary science or she was very pregnant. As time went on we began to speculate on the sire of the litter she carried. Toby, Pagan's brother, seemed to be favourite, for during the time when Omega had perked up a little I had taken her hunting with Toby and his owner Mick Kirby. We crated them together in my coffin-like trailer for an hour that night and while it seemed unlikely that Toby could have mated Omega while the trailer was travelling at fifty miles an hour on a bumpy terrain, he seemed the only choice. We continued to speculate and Omega continued to blow up like a balloon.

Well, the Thursday in question we hunted David's farm with a dozen or so terriers, including the very rotund Omega; and only after crating them and checking the pack for bites did Omega's changed shape become apparent. She was hours from whelping, so taking the heat lamp off Vampire who had recovered enough to be throwing himself against his shed door when another dog passed the kennels, I put Omega under the lamp and waited. Another hour would prove conclusively which dog had sired the litter.

To be a dog breeder, one needs to have a working knowledge of genetics and though I've heard numerous dumb-cluck dog breeders reiterate 'Genetics don't work with dogs,' all I can say is Gregor Mendel for all his pea fetish, has never let me down. If Omega had whelped a litter of Russell type puppies, the sire would have been Vampire. If one Toby type puppy, a self-tan of the type bred by Cyril Breay, had appeared in her litter, the sire would have been obvious. We waited and Omega began labour, finally passing a very large messy puppy which dutifully she cleaned and licked until we could discern it was a pale brindle. I sat admiring it and was about to race to the phone to tell Mick Toby had sired his first litter when she began labour once more and after a heck of a tussle finally passed another brindle, an enormous bull-terrier headed puppy, but there was something odd about the brindling, an odd dappling which looked unlike any brindling I had ever seen. I decided to wait for the third and last puppy, and when that was born, I had no doubt about the identity of the sire for the third puppy was marked like Omega and a blue merle in colour. It was baffling. Merle had, at that time, shown no interest in bitches, and in spite of much coaxing from David and other lurcher breeders, had failed to mate, and had been desperately ill nine weeks before the litter had been born. Furthermore there was no way I could see how Merle could have mated this bitch. Both had been kept in separate kennels, both had been almost too weak to stand at the time of conception.

I gave all the puppies away to friends as pets. It was a mistake, for the hunting qualities of both sire and dam manifested themselves in the puppies. The curious brindle which grew into a dun merle (an ugly colour) became a renowned cat killer in Aldridge, the sort of dog which sets my teeth on edge and alienates any neighbour who keeps livestock. The other brindle went to an old lady near Shenstone and vanishes for days to return, coat caked in mud and throat sliced by badger bites. The blue merle went to Keith Ruston, my photographer at that time. She grew into a tiny immaculately neat little terrier, attactive in spite of her undocked tail. Ruston had many offers to sell her, one too many as it happens, for one day a tinker boy turned up at the door of Ruston's house asking, 'Is der little dog for sale?', a statement I believe will herald the crack of Doomsday. She was gone the next night.

I had now no doubt as to the sire of Omega's litter.

The last hunt.

Epilogue

I've had thirteen happy years at David's place and though our rat scores don't exactly equal those of Dusaussois who zapped 16,050 in a month at Montfaucon abbatoir in 1840, I reckon I've set quite a record rat-wise. We sat down reading my diaries last week, and working on the average rat weighing 12 ounces, give or take a bit, I've taken seventy-eight tons of rats in thirteen years of hunting.

OK, so I've been bitten a few times and I've had thirteen short, sharp spells in hospital after sundry unpleasant bugs had made a concerted effort to carry me off, but you can't make omelettes without breaking eggs, can you? On the credit side—well, I've made nearly as many TV appearances as Tom and Jerry and numerous newspapers have photographed me live-catching rats, each photographer hoping and praying something would go wrong and he'll get a top-rate obituary to write (and it nearly came to that one night when a Dutch newspaper man photographed me getting bitten and a large rat trying to pull my hand into the hole).

They're tearing David's place down next week. We watched the valuers working out the price of equipment, loss of income and so on only yesterday. I've had thirteen glorious years there, and anyway, as my mother used to say, 'When one door closes another one opens'; but funnily enough I am totally resigned to the fact I'll never breed a bitch the equal of Omega.